Also by Shontaiye

All 4 Da Doe
Deceit, Lies, and Alibi's
Deceit, Lies, and Alibi's 2

Coming Soon by Shontaiye

Blood 4 My Brother
Wrong Turn
Thru the Eyes of a Hoodrat
Thru the Eyes of a Jackboy

Contact: Uptown Books:
uptownbookspublications.com (coming soon)
uptownbookspublication@yahoo.com

Contact: Shontaiye
uptownshontaiye@yahoo.com
https://twitter.com/LaRekaShontaiye
Instagram.com/shontaiye

All 4 Da Doe 2

SHONTAIYE

Uptown Books
1147 S. Salisbury Blvd
Suite 8-191
Salisbury, MD, 21801

This is a work of fiction. All of the characters, organizations, and events portrayed in this novel are either products of the author's imagination or are used fictitiously.

All 4 Da Doe.2 Copyright © 2015 Uptown Books. All rights reserved. No part of this book may be used or reproduced in any manner whatsoever without written permission except in the case of brief quotations embodied in critical articles or reviews.

ISBN-13-978-0-9863212-1-4
ISBN-10-0986321214

ACKNOWLEDGEMENTS

I would like to thank anyone that has actually read my book. I appreciate being given an opportunity as a new writer. I thank my mama for giving me feedback and reading through a lot of my crap before the final product is done.

ONE

FOUR MONTHS HAD passed since I found out my own sister was blackmailing me for money. I tried not to think about it, since at times it was hard to digest. I hadn't spoken to Briana since the day I had stormed out of her house, after finding account information that proved she was the cause of my unraveling life. It had taken everything out of me to keep from beating her ass half to death. The saying is very true: *Just because they're blood doesn't make them family.*

My Aunt Sheena, who had recently come back into our life, was still in contact with

Briana even though she had done what she had done. She refused to write her off, vowing to love her unconditionally. I too still loved her unconditionally, but I chose to love her with no contact. Some people you could have in your heart, but not in your life. And it would be a cold day in hell before she was allowed back in my life.

Ever since I was a girl, my life was heavily affected by the mistakes of others. I refused to let Briana's hatred and jealousy consume me or my life. I was a firm believer in choosing who you allowed into your circle and life, family or not.

As much as I disliked my sister at the time her true colors were revealed, I still chose to remain fair. There was no way in hell I was depositing a half a million in her account after I found out it was going to her and her shady ass boyfriend Eric. However, I did give her what she was entitled to: half. The scheming bitch damn sure wasn't getting a penny more.

Many people in a situation like ours would have just kept everything, and wouldn't have given her a dime. I on the other hand, wasn't like that. I believed in retribution. Even though I was wronged by my sister, eventually her guilt would eat away at her, and so would that bitch Karma.

The worst thing about the whole ordeal, was that our oldest sister Onney had ended up taking her life while we were being scammed by Briana. Unbeknownst to us, Onney had been on depression medications. Somehow her job found out she had been accessing prisoner information that we were using for our scam, and she was subsequently put under investigation. Onney knew shit was about to hit the fan, and took her life so she wouldn't have to face it.

Despite Onney committing suicide, Briana still continued her scheme during such a vulnerable time. She had no remorse even as Onney lay lying cold in her grave. The only reason she stopped was because she had been caught. Guilt still ate away at me every day about my role in Onney's death. I often wondered if it ate at Briana.

Layla suddenly appeared in the room and removed me from my not so fond memories.

"Mommy, you have a missed call from Aunt Sheena. I heard it ring but I couldn't get to it quick enough," Layla said, while extending the phone to me with her chubby hands. I took the phone quietly while she quickly scurried back to her room.

"Thanks baby," I replied, before she left. Looking down at the phone, I saw that I actually had *several* missed calls from Aunt Sheena. *I wonder what she wanted.* I dialed her number. The sound of her standard ringtone blared into my ears as I waited for her to answer the phone. After four rings she finally picked up.

"Hey Nina boo," my Aunt Sheena greeted me warmly in the receiver. "I almost missed your call, I was washing my hands." I could hear the warm smile in her voice, as well as the water still running in the background.

"Wassup with you Auntie? Everything ok?" I asked.

"Just callin to check up on you and Lay." She paused as if she wanted to say something but was hesitant. "I saw Briana. She called me, and I met her after work. I figured you wouldn't want her around the house," she said, referring to my studio apartment she lived in.

I remained silent. After-all, Aunt Sheena was praying for a response that I was not about to give her.

"Nina when you gon at least sit down and talk to Briana? At least to get some damn answers? Don't you want to know what the hell was going on inside her head when she did what she did? I'm not saying you have to kiss and make up, I'm just saying that something terribly wrong happened and she owes you an explanation. Then you can move on. I know you love your sister. You two share a bond."

"Is she still with Eric?" I asked, rolling my eyes and disregarding the speech she just gave. I didn't want to hear the sermon right now.

"She says she's still seeing him, but she is trying to get her life back on track. I know what I'm about to tell you doesn't make it any better, but Briana also struggled with depression. She never told you, but she was on meds too. You know like she does, going from foster home to foster home wasn't easy. She felt abandoned and she felt unloved. I feel guilty that the two of you had to go through that...I understand it. That's why I try to support her through whatever she's going through…Briana always said, and now I see, that you were always the strong one and that's why you became the most successful, even without the illegal shit."

As much as I hated to, I went ahead and told Aunt Sheena what we had been involved with and Briana's blackmail. When shit hit the fan, and after learning of my sisters' betrayal, I had to confide in someone. My aunt seemed like the perfect person to do so with. As terrible as it may seem, I had tried to take something negative and make it positive. I bought a few rental homes, made stock and bond investments, and now I was financially stable. It wasn't my fault that Briana didn't do the same. We split everything down the middle. She had no right to envy me, and make me accountable for the choices she had made.

As a child I was weak and helpless, and in and out of foster homes. I refused to be that way as an adult, and that was simply a choice I had consciously made. Briana had a choice as well, so I wasn't budging on my stance on the matter, nor my cold attitude towards her.

"I understand that Aunt Sheena, but it's hard to empathize with that because she crossed her family. Me out of all people." I paused. "She sent someone to my home to muscle me. Do you know how terrified I was? I even sold my house. And the most fucked up thing out of all this shit is, Onney is dead. She took her life. Regardless of the fact of her being depressed, Briana's bullshit added to it. It sent her over the edge. Did Briana stop after that? No. She kept going on with it. I cried on that bitch's shoulders over *our* sister and she didn't care. So Aunt Sheena, I love you, and I mean no disrespect, but fuck Briana," I said harshly.

Aunt Sheena sat silently on the phone for a minute, and I didn't hear anything but her breathing. She finally responded. "Nina just give it some thought. I do want to say that nobody is perfect. I've made some bad choices I'm ashamed of too. I've hurt some loved ones as well. I know what Bri is going through, because I've personally been there. If you don't do it for her, do it for me. Even if it's later in the future," she said.

"I'll think on it Aunt Sheena," I finally said, insincerely. A lot had happened and I wasn't exactly sure how to fix it. I wasn't the one who should be trying to fix it.

One thing for sure, I wasn't going to make any promises to anyone.

TWO

THE NEXT DAY I thumbed through, and carefully reviewed a stack of papers I had received from one of the Claims Rep's at Aetna. Things were going great at my job since I had been recently promoted to a Supervisor in the Fraud Department. The irony right... The position came with a $15,000 raise, and the perk of being able to work from home. Working from home allowed me to continue work on expanding my property business during prime hours. Of course I couldn't let it interfere with my work for Aetna, but I was the queen of multi-tasking so I was succeeding.

So far, I had four new boarding house properties, with plans to buy two more properties within the next six months. That would bring my total to ten units, and produce income of around $8,000 per month, after expenses such as electric, water, and maintenance. At that rate, I would no longer have to use my savings to grow. I could use income produced from the room rentals to buy a new property every three months. My goal was to have around twenty rooming house properties in three years. I had no doubt in my mind that I could do it, especially since I was making good money at Aetna, lived below my means, and had a nice savings to rely on.

I glanced over at the clock and saw that it was close to twelve, so I decided to take a lunch break and get some fresh air. I had been sitting still since eight, and I needed a good stretch. I grabbed my favorite brown Coach bag, and threw on my lightweight, Polo jacket. I had a taste for crab dip and bruschetta, so I hopped in my Mustang for the ten minute drive to Brick House Tavern.

After returning with my overpriced crab

dip, I plopped down in my faux leather office chair and swung my feet up onto my steel filing cabinet. Right after getting comfortable, I immediately began digging into my crab dip, while savoring the rich blend of crab meat, cream, and cheeses. While reaching over and grabbing my phone, I noticed I had several missed calls from Rashid, and a text message from my male friend Naseef. Quickly navigating through my phone, I read the message from Naseef:

> *"Hey sexy, you got some time for me tonight? Miss you and wanna hang out."*

I smiled at the thought of Naseef. I had met him months ago through Briana, before our falling out. We had been at the bookstore, Black and Nobel in North Philly, when he walked in. Briana had spoken to him, saying she knew him. The whole time I stared discreetly in awe. He was a beautiful manly sight. He stood around six feet, and had a medium build, but was toned like he lifted weights. He had a low cut and smelled sweet, yet masculine. He had hood swag that was displayed by smoke black Timberland boots, and Levi jeans that actually fit. His face was an average handsome, but the aura that he generated was not.

After he caught me staring, he introduced himself and extended his hand for me to shake. When I reached my hand out, he wrapped his hands around mine and brought it up to his lips, placing a slow kiss on it. I blushed and smiled sweetly, while pulling my hand away. I introduced myself as Briana's sister, and he continued to follow us around the store, while we shopped for books. On our way out, he stopped me and asked could he rap to me for a second, without Briana. Briana knew the game and scurried to the car, leaving me and Naseef alone.

We exchanged numbers, and I had spoken to him sporadically until recently. After Briana and I became estranged I found myself yearning for companionship. Of course I still had Rashid, but everyone in my life so far, had let me down, including Rashid. I figured it was time I have some fun and get to know Naseef. I didn't want anything long term, I just wanted his company and some excitement to wake up my dull life. No doubt, somewhere in me still loved Rashid, but I had to remind myself that love wasn't enough to stop him from shitting on me multiple times. Needless to say, I wasn't going to put all my eggs in that basket. Besides, I was focused on my daughter, my business, and my job at Aetna. In that order.

Later that evening, I parked my car and stepped out wearing black leggings, a fitted gold top and peep toe, split front booties. I looked very sexy, with my curvy body stretching the fabric. The gold top gave my chocolate skin an exotic glow while the tights looked like they had been painted on. I checked myself in my compact mirror, before applying more lip gloss to my full lips. I confirmed I was cute, and then made my way to the entrance of Houlihans to meet Naseef for dinner.

The restaurant was in Plymouth Meeting, which was about a thirty minute drive from my house, depending on the traffic. When I entered, I immediately spotted Naseef waving for me from a small booth in a dimly lit corner. I made my way to him and greeted him with a warm hug.

"Hey Doll. How are you?" I grinned, inhaling his signature sweet scent. *Damn he was fine. He could definitely get it.*

"I'm good baby. Glad you could come out. And happy you didn't stand me up like you did the last couple of times," he reminded me. He motioned for me to take a seat.

I dismissed the comment and sat my jacket down beside me in the booth. Smiling flirtatiously, I leaned forward and responded. "So what's on the agenda tonight?" I asked, while staring into his handsome face. I was extremely attracted to this man.

"Oh, what you got the whole night out?" he asked, his eyebrows raising up in curiosity.

"Something like that," I replied, pushing my long hair being my shoulder.

Layla was hanging out with her dad since

it was Friday night. He had been working at his job for almost a year, so when he asked to go on day-shift it was immediately approved since there was an opening. It worked well for everyone, with Rashid being able to spend more time with Layla, even seeing her more during the week. He even had a car, so I didn't have to be the one taking her back and forth.

He was no longer staying at my home as much, since Rashid, even though a street nigga, was known to be clingy and very jealous.

I had tightened up on allowing him to stay with us. Coping with my sister's death had become easier, and I now felt safer since I had moved out of the old house right after my falling out with Briana. I had no idea who she had sent over to my home that dreadful night, and I wasn't going to stick around for them to ever come back.

I ended up renting a modest three-bedroom apartment in a nice gated community in Willow Grove. It took me some time to sell my townhouse so I wasn't rushing into another mortgage. I was saving a lot of money living in the apartment, and Layla enjoyed the amenities that came with it like the pool. I personally enjoyed the security. No one was getting through those gates, and visitors had to provide proper identification to get into the community.

I looked up at Naseef who was waving his hand in front of my face.

"Earth to Nina," he said with a grin, while still waving.

I smiled. I had been thinking. "Yeah I'll take a Long Island Iced Tea," I finally replied. I would also need a shot afterward. I was just getting started.

Naseef had been asking me what I wanted to drink. He should've been asking, *how many drinks do you want?* For the past few months I had been drinking almost every night. I usually didn't get drunk, but it was certainly more than I had ever drank before.

The liquor helped me sleep at night, and it helped me think less about the situation with Briana. When I was in work mode I was so sure of myself, so confident and poised; however, when it came to relationships, whether it was Rashid, Briana, or Aunt Sheena, it had at one point been dysfunctional. All of these people had let me down multiple times at some point in the past. It was scary hoping that it wouldn't happen again, but in my mind I knew it probably would. The alcohol was a temporary getaway from life's stress. It wasn't healthy, but hey, it is what it is.

For the next half hour, Naseef and I talked and laughed over a table full of mainly appetizers. We had so much chemistry and he was very easy to talk to. Several times I had to suppress the dirty thoughts I was having about him.

"So Nina, could you see yourself with a nigga like me?" Naseef asked out of the blue. His eyes were glossy from the liquor, but he was serious.

"I mean you smart and got ya shit together. You seem like you go for a different type of dude." Naseef stared at me waiting for a response. Watching me intently he proceeded to stuff a fried butterfly shrimp in his mouth, while flicking the breading crumbs from his fingers into the napkin.

Finally responding, I said, "Believe it or not, I'm a sucker for a street dude. It's just something about their presence and the aura they give off. I mean with me, as long as a man is extremely masculine and is a good provider, I'm open."

"Really?" he asked, eyebrows going up again. It appeared to be a habit of his when he was curious. He took another gulp of his double shot of vodka and looked to me for a response.

"I mean when I was younger I was attracted to the guys in the street, but clearly most of them weren't husband material. Now as an adult, I'm still attracted to that kind of dude but all the street shit has to be in the past. So a matured street nigga," I joked, laughing.

"So what type of work you do?" I asked Naseef, turning the conversation to him. We had talked about me enough. I smeared sour cream on top of my loaded potato skin and took a bite.

"Me, I work as a supervisor at the trash company down South West Philly," he stated proudly.

"That's good," I exclaimed, highly surprised. Naseef had the hood written all over him literally, with tattoos up his arms and around his neck. It was always good to see young men try to make something of themselves even when the jobs seemed menial to the world.

"I'm not even gon lie to you tho, I do my thing very quietly. I mean I'm thankful for my job. Very. But things get expensive when you trying to get away from the neighborhoods you grew up in," he confessed, with a serious look on his face.

I knew it was more to it, I thought. *The nigga drives a new Benz for goodness sakes.* I didn't know what he meant by he did his thing. For all I know he could be robbing on the side or dealing dope, but I damn sure wasn't going to ask. This wasn't a confessional booth, and I wasn't trying to get deep.

"Well I definitely understand. I don't judge anybody on how they get it, cuz believe me, I'm no Saint. The most important thing is to make it count for something. If you're going to risk your life and freedom, make it worth it," I said, giving my free two cents.

"Trust me baby. I definitely do," he reassured me.

We ended the night by going to see the new horror movie AnnaBelle. He wanted to continue the evening but the liquor had hit me and I wasn't going to wait around to let it hit me harder. When it did, I wanted to be somewhere familiar.

While dropping me back off to my car I told Naseef I would call him, additionally he made me promise to see him for lunch on Friday. He wanted to meet during the week but he worked twelve hour shifts Monday through Thursday, and I wasn't going to play myself by staying out super late, so I would be tired and unproductive in the morning. Business always came first.

Ending the night, I gave him a kiss that lasted a little longer than expected. I can't lie, the nigga had my pussy throbbing and I didn't want to go. However, I did the responsible, safe thing and carried my ass home before I wound up bent over somewhere with his dick stuck in me. Lately the liquor had me feeling extra horny.

Before I pulled off, I checked my phone to discover that Rashid had called me again. He had called me twice in the restaurant but I had ignored him since I knew he didn't want shit. If it was important he would have surely texted me the issue by now. I dialed him back.

"Hey wassup. You called?" I said, asking the rhetorical question.

"Yeah, just seeing if you was okay. Where you at anyway?" he asked.

"I went out with a friend. And Rashid you don't have to call me five times to see if I'm okay. What's Layla doing?"

"Yeah aight. Who you go with Asia?" he asked disregarding the comment, as well as my question. He was being nosey. He already knew that if I said I was with Asia, it would be a lie and I wouldn't give him the satisfaction of thinking I had to lie to him.

"Na a friend, you don't know them," I said, dismissing the topic. "What's Layla doing, sleeping?" I asked again.

"Yeah. We played monopoly and then went to get some water ice from Rita's. She fell asleep in the car on the way back. Why don't you stay with us tonight?" Rashid asked, abruptly changing the subject again. He was comical.

"Naaa, I'm tired and I'm about to head home." The alcohol I had consumed was steadily creeping up on me and I already knew that going over to Rashid's would lead to fucking. It always did. Rashid knew exactly what he was doing.

"Why don't you just come over here tho? I stay closer than you, and I can hear your voice slurring from the alcohol. You can't be out there drunk driving and shit. Think of Layla," Rashid said laying it on thick, and forcing me to evaluate my decision to drive all the way home.

Exhaling deeply, I agreed. "Aight, you right. I'll be there in about fifteen minutes." I started my car up and hopped on Germantown Pike to take the drive down to Rashid's, in the Germantown section of Philadelphia. I was feeling horny anyway so I didn't mind. I made sure to take my time to avoid being pulled over.

By the time I got to Rashid's building I was incredibly relaxed and on cloud nine.

I parked my car in the quiet parking lot and walked the fifteen feet along the side of the building to his apartment door. Before I could even knock, Rashid opened the door. The nigga must have been looking out the window.

"Wassup?" he asked, with a serious look on his handsome, brown face.

"Hey." I responded quietly, while greeting him with a smile. I kicked off my heels at the door and followed Rashid to the living room. He plopped down on the chocolate brown sectional, picked up the controller to his video game, and proceeded to play Fight Night. I sat on the opposite side of the chair and got comfortable.

"You want something to drink?" Rashid asked, picking up a cup from off the coffee table to take a sip. I hadn't detected he had been drinking on the phone when I spoke to him. Had I noticed the slur I wouldn't had come by. He always did the most when he was drunk.

"Na, I'm good." I already knew what

Rashid was up to. Every time he started drinking he wanted to fuck and get on some emotional nigga shit. I didn't mind fucking him, it's just that Rashid wanted more than what I was willing to give at the moment. He was used to the past Nina who was head over heels for him, not the older Nina who could separate emotions from a good dick down. It wasn't my fault; his ass made me that way.

"Yeah I know, you already on," he stated sarcastically, with a weird look on his face. *Here we go with this emotional drunk shit. Throwing shade,"* I thought to myself.

"Yeah," I replied, nonchalant, with a grin, not saying what I really had in mind.

"Where you say you go again?" he asked for the second time, while glancing over at me suspiciously.

"I already told you Rashid. And wassup with the twenty one questions?" I asked, growing irritated.

"I'm just asking. You play a lot of games Nina." Rashid stared at me briefly, and then shook his head and turned his focus back to his game.

"Yeah aight Rashid. I didn't come over to argue with you about what I do on my spare time. Cuz frankly, it's my business. You worried about who I'm with and on some real shit, worried about who I'm fuckin," I said bluntly, with a straight face and no emotion. I cared about Rashid, but wasn't going there with him. I had to hide my emotions with him because once he saw it, he would use it as a weakness.

He grew irritated and smacked his teeth in frustration. "One minute you act like you tryin to make sumn work with us, and the next minute you running around being secretive," he snapped. He paused the game and lay the controller down to turn and face me.

Screwing up my face in disbelief, I asked, "Cuz we fuck? Cuz we fuck I gotta be tryin to make sumn work?... U fucked bitches all the time you claimed you didn't give a fuck about, so that's dead Rashid," I said bringing up the past.

"I'm not gon argue with you. That's not what I came here for. It's Saturday night, I work over fifty hours a week and the last thing

I'ma do is fuck up my night arguing. And you really need to relax on the drinking when you have Layla," I said, hypocritically. Yeah, I had a drink or two when Layla was home, but I wasn't emotional and erratic when I drank.

He shot me a funny look and said, "Aren't you the one to talk. And anyway she's sleep and I worked all day too, so I'm relaxing," he said with an attitude.

Rolling my eyes, I got up off the chair and went to the fridge to get the drink Rashid had originally offered. I had to drown his ass out, just like I did everything else. He was about to get the silent treatment in his own home. I don't understand why the nigga wanted to argue about "us" every time he got drunk. At the end of the night he still would get the same response.

His real problem was he couldn't dictate what I did, and who I did it with. He didn't want to hear I was fucking, but he was acting like that's what he wanted me to confess to. Sad thing was I wasn't fucking anyone but him, *yet*. I knew he loved me at the end of the day, but when you love someone you should do right. I wasn't about to play myself again, so I would continue to ignore his child-like tantrums.

Still standing in the kitchen, I pulled out the opened bottle of Hennessey, and poured me a shot. I quickly swallowed the foul tasting Cognac and walked to the back of the apartment to take a quick shower. I wasn't worried about clothes since I would just throw back on what I came in, minus the panties of course.

When I came out I peeped into the spare bedroom used as Layla's room, and saw that she was sprawled out wildly, still sleeping. I noticed the room now had pink curtains and that Rashid had put in a little dresser and TV for her. I smiled. He really was trying. *Maybe I was wrong about him.*

The cognac I had drank settled in nicely to my surprise, since I usually didn't mix my liquors. The high I felt from the nights alcohol had me super faded. I walked back into the living room still damp, and boldly stood in front of Rashid. Dropping the thick, blue towel I was wrapped in, I acted like nothing ever happened, and we weren't just bickering twenty minutes ago. I wasn't into games and this is what he really wanted anyway. Besides, I too wanted it in the worse way. I didn't say a word to Rashid; I just waited.

He ignored me for five seconds and then turned the T.V off, peering up at me with glassy, alcohol infused eyes. Grabbing me by my waist, he pulled my naked body down into his lap and kissed my neck gently, then my forehead. Looking directly into my eyes, he asked, "Nina, why you playing games, huh? You know I love you." *The liquor was talking*.

I didn't bother to respond. I just kissed him and then slowly rose up. I was drunk and horny and I just wanted him to do what he did best: eat my pussy and fuck me good. I pushed him back, unbuckled his pants and pulled out his swollen dick. I skillfully and hungrily took him in my mouth. Once again, I blame it on the liquor. Had I been sober he definitely wouldn't be getting his dick sucked. But lately, I was always on, so he was being spoiled. Rashid moaned and squirmed while I sucked, slurped and licked. When I was done getting him rock hard, he reciprocated, and I came the same way I always did.

The next morning I rose quickly out of Rashid's warm bed, leaving silently. I didn't want Layla to wake up with me there. She was getting older and I didn't want to confuse her. Seeing me there she would think we would be getting back together. If it didn't work, she would be crushed. I had given it some thought, but I just wasn't ready. I did care about Rashid, I just didn't have time to pour everything into him again.

For as long as I could remember, I'd always been everyone's rock: the strong one. I was tired of that. I just wanted to be free; free from disappointment. Rashid has let me down multiple times, and Briana drove a stake through my heart with her betrayal. Onney's death had also taken a toll on me. I didn't want anyone to use my shoulders anymore, especially since the only thing that was keeping them up through the day, was a bottle of vodka at night.

THREE

MONDAY CAME FASTER than expected as usual. The beginning of the week I was usually stuck on the phone and swamped in papers to review, but today I found myself on the phone with my realtor Nate. Nate worked for a real estate company in downtown Philadelphia, and was helping me acquire properties cheaply throughout the city. He had called me to inform me about some cheap homes in the Strawberry Mansion section of the city. The area was up and coming and wasn't as popular for rooming houses. According to Nate, these properties were more profitable to flip and resell.

Figuring it could be a good opportunity to make some larger, quicker cash, I decided to find out more, so I agreed to stop by Nate's office around eleven. I would review the stack of possible fraudulent claims later tonight. That was the beauty of working home.

The ride downtown went by pretty quickly thanks to the absence of rush hour traffic, and the soothing voice of John Legend professing his love in *All of Me*. When I got to my destination, I stepped out looking like business. My Remi hair was bone straight against the black Ralph Lauren wrap dress I wore. I kept it simple, only wearing gold studs, and a gold cross I never took off. I looked very polished, yet stylish since I had on my white leather, split, peep toe booties by Gianvito Rossi. The shoes were sick and contrasted beautifully against the black. They'd set me back $700, but that was a secret splurge of mine I wouldn't tell anyone.

When I got my money all the way up, I planned to buy a new Audi Q5 SUV to complete my overall look. I wasn't one of those people who liked to fraud, so for now I would stay in my lane with my Mustang. It was good enough for now, allowing me to still look somewhat classy while I conducted business.

I parked my car at the attended lot around the corner, and after getting my ticket from the attendant, I took the two minute walk to the narrow, congested Chestnut Street. I entered the glass double doors of Nate's building, and was immediately greeted by the front desk clerk. After signing the visitor log, I made my way up to the fifth floor. I was always amazed at how much the downtown retail space cost when the buildings appeared to be so basic. As I walked into Suite 505, I was greeted again by a more familiar face.

"Good morning Miss Washington, how are you?" Gina asked, with a warm smile.

"I am fabulous. How've you been," I asked. Gina the receptionist, was one of my favorite people at CT Realty. She was the stereotypical blonde; blue eyed and bubbly.

"I'm wonderful," she said cheerfully. "Haven't seen you in a while and glad you're back. You can go ahead back. Nate's expecting you," she said. With her headset already on, she quickly punched in Nate's extension to let him know I was headed into his office. He was standing at the door before I made it back.

"Hey Nina!" Nate said brightly, showing his perfect white teeth. He was a very handsome white man in his forties, but didn't look a day over thirty-five. He always dressed nice, and was great to do business with since he was very straightforward.

"Hey Nate. How are you?" I asked, returning a smile.

"Great! Ready to get some of that cash in your pocketbook!" he joked, still flashing his mega-watt smile. Like I said, he was very straightforward, yet still charismatic and charming.

"First you have to talk some numbers and show me some pictures," I said, sitting down into the comfortable, royal blue office chair. I was ready to get down to business.

"Of course," he said. He walked around his large, mahogany desk and pulled out some photos and passed them to me.

"So getting down to business, there's two

properties I think you'll be interested in, right in the Strawberry Mansion section of the city. The price is phenomenal, and the area is up and coming. Now they will definitely need some work, but once that's done you could easily double your money by reselling them. I wouldn't room these houses out; they're not large enough and there's not as much of a market for it in this family oriented area."

I looked through the pictures and saw potential, but wasn't impressed. One had a gaping hole in the wall, and the other looked like it would need a whole new kitchen and bathroom.

"What's the price?" I asked, finally looking up from the pictures.

"$14,900 a piece, but I believe I can help you get them both for $20,000. The owners are motivated and right now this is a buyer's market. The best part is if you put $10,000 in each house, you could easily see a return of at least $40,000. Spend forty, get back $80,000 easy. And of course, I'll help you sell them."

I sat silently for a moment while I contemplated the idea. I had been focusing on renting rooms, so I never thought about actually flipping homes. To me it was risky, but the price was hard to beat and it could be extremely profitable if done properly.

I looked up at Nate, who was now seated on the other side of his desk waiting for a response.

"Put in my offer. If I fix these houses up you better sell them for me Nate," I said seriously. "I don't want to lose forty grand."

Even though I had the money, I wasn't into taking losses. At the end of the day, this was business. I made a mental note to do more research on the area. If it wasn't what he said, I would rescind my offer.

"You'll never lose Nina, because even if I couldn't sell them, which I know I can, and will, you could rent them out. So you don't lose," he replied confidently.

"So you want to swing over and take a look at them," he asked. "I can tell you my vision, I can show you some price comp's for the area and we can get started on the paperwork. I'm trying to get this deal done while it's still hot," he laughed, before hopping up from his chair.

"Let's go. I have a few hours," I said, before getting up to follow Nate out the door.

A few days had passed since my meeting with Nate and since I was paying cash, the closing process was going by quickly and easily. After seeing the properties and hearing Nate's vision, I felt confident with my decision to buy. I had already begun discussing the rehab process with my contractors and had several meetings scheduled to go over what needed to be done. While we were over in Strawberry Mansion looking at the house, Nate had also shown me a gigantic Victorian house that could be converted into four units: three two bedrooms, and a one bedroom. The price was jaw dropping, and with some renovation, could bring excellent long-term income. Hell, I could probably even resell it for a staggering price. I was ready to go ham on investing, but I can't lie, it was wearing me out with my regular workload.

Rubbing my tired eyes, I continued to look over some paperwork I had been emailed. I was playing catch-up from the days before. My job at Aetna was pretty easy and straightforward. I basically made sure my team was handling fraudulent claims properly. Any they had trouble with, or any that weren't as clear, came to me.

Lately there had been a lot more than expected. Since the fraud identifying process was so intricate, it took a lot of time before we were able to label it as actual fraud. Each claim took several hours of review and usually was a build-up of past fraudulent issues. Unfortunately for me, I had about ten on my desk that weren't clear. It would be a long month at this rate.

"Mommy," Layla called. "What time are we eating?" she asked.

Looking up from my work I glanced at the time. *Shit*. It was after eight. Clearly I had lost track of time.

"I'm sorry honey," I said to Layla, who was standing by the door. "I lost track of time. It's too late to cook. I'll order something. You choose."

"Okay!" she replied excitedly. I usually cooked meals at home, even if it was a bagged, pre-made, skillet meal. Takeout would certainly be a treat for her.

A half hour later we sat on the sofa eating Chinese food. Layla had requested Kung Pao Chicken, which I had never eaten before. She said she had heard someone in school talking about it and wanted to stray from our normal Beef and Broccoli or General Tso's chicken. It actually was pretty tasty.

"So Mom, the sleepover is tomorrow night. Were you going to drop me off, or was my dad going to?" she asked, between forkfuls of food. Of course I had forgotten her daycare was having a sleepover for the older girls at the center, sort of like a girl's night.

"Oh shoot! I forgot about the sleepover," I said, slapping my forehead. I can take you. I don't have anywhere to be."

"Ok. I told my dad too. He sounded a little sad that I wouldn't be spending the night with him like usual. I told him we still had Saturday," she said seriously.

I smiled at her comment. Rashid had been doing a really good job with Layla. I wish he had the same mentality when we were together, however, I always have to remind myself that we both were very young at that time

"I'm sure he'll be okay honey. Go ahead and finish up your food, so you can brush your teeth and get to bed. I don't want you tired in the morning."

It was now nine thirty and she had to be up early. I on the other hand, would be up for several more hours working on claims. I was going to text Naseef later and cancel our Friday night date. I just had entirely too much work to do.

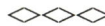

Thank god it's Friday, I thought, as I looked over to the clock on my desk the following day. Unfortunately, it was only 10 o clock and the day had just begun. I had been pretty productive so far, settling two claims. My goal was to have another one done before lunch. I

had a meeting with my contractor at 12:45 to give him a deposit on the work he was going to do for me. I had settled quickly on the properties in Strawberry Mansion, and estimated repairs to be done in four to six weeks.

I had my hands full for sure with eight occupied rooming houses and two renovations underway. I was seriously considering hiring someone to help me out. Passive income wasn't always passive. Luckily for me, none of my tenants that rented rooms from me had any complaints, and everything at my houses were working fine.

With the ways things were going, I was expecting to see an estimated income of $11,000 per month. It was modest income, but it was excellent rental property income. That figure didn't include my two unit, duplex flip which Nate said he could price aggressively at $60,000 each, which was much more than what I expected. I stood to make at least $50,000 cash off that one flip. That could be more if I kept material costs low. Ultimately, if the process went smooth and the sale was a success, then I was going to add flipping houses to my portfolio also.

After receiving and making over a dozen phone calls, I was tired of looking at claims and dealing with properties. It was just my luck that by the middle of the day, the damn water heater broke at my unit that Aunt Sheena lived in. I had spoken too soon and jinxed myself. How the hell that happened, I have no idea since I bought it new from Sears.

After sitting on the phone with Sears customer service and calling my contractor, I had to rearrange my schedule and run down to North Philly to check out the situation. There was also some water that had leaked from the heater, and if it had caused any damage, Sears and I were going to have a problem. It was going to be a long stressful day dealing with all the madness around me, but this was only *part* of what I wanted. I wanted the big bucks, and everyone knows, that always comes with a price.

Lying peacefully in my tub, I reached over and grabbed the drink that was sitting on the edge of the tub by my shoulder. I swirled the round, bowl shaped glass around before I took a gulp of the familiar to put my body at ease. The pale yellow liquid had only a drop of orange juice. These days, I was using more and more vodka. The fluid went down my throat smoothly. I continued to soak until I heard my phone vibrating on the floor. I reached over quickly, splashing a little bit of water. I thought it might be Layla, whom I had taken to the daycare at seven for the sleepover. To my surprise, it was Naseef.

"Hello," I said, after pushing the accept button on my iPhone.

"Wassup Nina?" Naseef asked.

"Nothing much, relaxing in the tub. I had a long ass day," I said. I didn't go into my business too much with Naseef. You never know what people will do for the dough. I had learned that the hard way.

"Damn. Wish I could join you, or you at least join me. I know you said you had been busy and was tired, but I aint tryin to stress you. We can chill, have a drink, get some food. Sumn laid back so you can relax. What you think about that?" he asked.

I ain't gon lie, it sounded good, and the liquor had me feeling good so I agreed. I told him I would be a couple of hours. I had to get dressed and drive to Northeast Philadelphia and I didn't want to rush while he waited. We made plans to meet at Chickie's and Pete's on Roosevelt Boulevard. Wasn't nothing like some good ass hot wings with a glass of vodka and pineapple.

I ended up getting dressed quicker than I thought. I stood in my full length mirror and admired my appearance. I had on an all-black jumpsuit with a deep V that came to my waist. My chocolate, C-cup breasts were slightly, but tastefully exposed, while my bone straight blend-in weave, flowed seductively to the top of my round ass. Hands down, I looked good. I piled on some raspberry colored lip-gloss from Lancome, and headed out the door.

Before jumping into my car, I called Layla to make sure she was okay. Of course she was having fun at the sleepover, painting nails and blabbering with her little girlfriends. After speaking with her, I called Naseef to let him know I was on the way. To my surprise, he wasn't answering. By the time I got ahold of him, I was almost on the Boulevard.

"Yo!" Naseef yelled into the receiver over the massive amount of background noise.

"Hey. I've been calling you. I'm about to get on the Boulevard, where are you? Sounds like you're in a bar," I said, yelling into the phone like he was, so he could hear me.

"Damn, you said two hours so I figured I had time to have a couple drinks with some of my niggas. But that's cool. You close by. Swing thru here and we can take my car. You said you was tired anyway. I can drive," he offered.

"I don't know about that Naseef. I aint trying to leave my car in North Philly." The gesture was nice but that idea was dead. I wasn't knew to this shit. A crackhead would be digging through my shit within ten minutes.

"Aight, well come through real quick. We can have a drink here and I'll say bye to my man."

"Aight cool. Where you at?" I asked. I

didn't have a problem meeting him real quick since I did come earlier than expected.

"The Eagles Bar," he replied, still loud as hell.

Frowning my face up, I pulled the phone away from my ear and stared at it. This nigga was tripping. He expected me to come to the center of the damn hood, on Erie Avenue. Here I was dolled all up, and he wanted me to come right into a den of thirsty ass niggas, and hating ass broads.

"You gotta be kidding me?" I asked in disbelief. "I'm not trying to come off as bourgeois or nothing, but I came out for you, and you want me to come to the damn Eagle's Bar? Shit, Chickie's and Pete's aint glamorous but it's down Northeast, not North Philly."

"Chill,..I got you. I'ma be ten minutes. Promise. And I'll meet you outside. You know niggas gon be tryin to get at ya sexy ass and I ain't having that," he said.

Smacking my teeth, I agreed and altered my route, eventually ending up on the busy, ghetto block of Germantown and Erie.

◇◇◇

"Damnnn, what's your name sis? Can I get to know you?" was all I heard walking up Germantown Avenue to the corner of Erie. The two bars that were side by side caused limited parking, and I found myself forced further down the block than expected. Naseef met me about a quarter of the way, and boy was I glad; the niggas was thirsty. They acted like they never saw a decent looking bitch before. Of course, the looks and the hate of the hood dust-bunnies started before I could even put my custom made, rhinestone heel in the door. I wasn't worried tho. I had class, but I wouldn't hesitate to lay hands on any bitch that got out of line. I was from the hood too.

Taking a seat at the crowded bar, I ordered my favorite drink, a Long Island Iced Tea. Luckily Naseef knew the bartender so I didn't have to flag her ass down. She was a cute younger girl and had her shiny lips pursed together with an attitude. Despite the attitude I still gave her a tip, even though the only tip I should've given her was don't wear fuckin faux, fur eyelashes. The shit looked ridiculous along with the makeup she had caked on. *This is why they hate. Take some time and get yaself right instead of eyeballing the next bitch cuz she look good,* I thought to myself, as I nursed my glass.

Naseef continued to talk to his two friends. He called himself introducing me in the crowded bar, but of course that was a fail. One of the guys looked a little familiar, and I take it he felt the same, since he kept glancing at me. He called himself doing it discreetly, but I peeped it. Keeping his word, after ten minutes Naseef was ready and we headed out. As I exited the door my heart suddenly dropped. *Here we go with the bullshit,* I thought.

FOUR

Rashid was talking to his friend but stopped mid-sentence when he saw me coming out the Eagle's Bar. I cursed myself for bringing my ass out there when I knew he was born and raised in North Philadelphia. This was his stomping ground, and I was outta line. At the end of the day I was a big girl, and I could do what I want, but I was playing with fire since I knew Rashid was in his feelings and I continued to fuck him. It wasn't fair, but that's what it was.

"Yo, what the fuck?" Rashid immediately snarled, while giving me the "ice grill." Of course he hadn't bother to say hello, instead reacting off emotion. I ain't gon lie, he was looking good as hell; unfortunately the scowl on his face fucked that all up.

I wasn't really sure what to say; I didn't want to go at it with Rashid in front of that many people.

"Let me holla at you real fast Nina," he said, not really asking. He waved his hand for me to come with him, and immediately walked off without looking back to see if I was actually coming. I looked at Naseef, and whispered, "Please let me handle this alone." He seemed hesitant but eventually agreed.

I slowly followed behind Rashid to keep things from escalating. Rashid was an emotional hothead and things could get out of pocket real quick. I knew Naseef was from the hood too, and I didn't want a damn Mexican standoff. I continued around the corner to talk to Rashid. Exiting Erie avenue, we navigated onto Germantown Avenue to a closed store so we could talk.

"Yo, what the fuck you doing down here Nina?" he asked, visibly pissed, but still trying to control the volume of his voice. Anger was written on his face.

"I stopped by for a drink. What's the problem?" I asked, unintentionally pushing his buttons more. I had my arms crossed against my body, trying my best to act innocent.

"Stop fucking lying--You stopped by for a drink dressed like that? Tight ass clothes, titties popping out, ass on display for all of North Philly?" he asked, getting up in my face. I took a step back but my back quickly met the wall.

"Yep." That's all I could say as Rashid grew angrier with each word I spoke.

"Oh yeah?" he asked, now nose to nose with me. I could smell the alcohol on his breath and hear the malice in his voice.

"Back the fuck up Rashid, I'm not doing this shit with you," I said, growing fearful. I extended my hand out, forcing him to back up some.

"I ain't gotta do shit. I should knock ya fucking head off out here," he growled. "You was bout to leave with that fuck ass nigga. Where was you going Nina? Ready to run off and suck some fucking dick?" he accused, looking me up and down with his face turned up. The comment amused me just a little, but nevertheless, it was highly disrespectful.

"First of all, don't worry about me Rashid. We aint together. If I want to stop by and have a drink with a friend, then that's my business. And furthermore, the theatrics is getting old, and I ain't fuckin with you like that no more. Our conversations will be limited to our daughter. I don't have time for this nut shit," I said, with an attitude, before attempting to walk off.

"Naaa. Go the fuck home Nina. You not leaving wit no nigga while I'm out here," he said, roughly grabbing my arm, and attempting to drag me to my car.

"Get the fuck off me Rashid!" I yelled, while attempting to break free from his iron-clad grip.

"Yo stop fuckin playing with me, before I beat ya ass out here," he threatened. Rashid wasn't typically violent with me, but tonight I guess he'd had enough of my games. I didn't give a fuck though, since he put me through more bullshit then imaginable.

Forcefully dragging me down the street, I pleaded with Rashid to release my arm. Right before reaching the car, I heard a familiar voice calling me from down the street. It was Naseef.

"Nina baby, you alright?" he asked, while cautiously walking up the street towards me and Rashid. People were watching now, and I was praying Rashid's ass didn't make more of a scene.

Giving me a dirty look before releasing my arm, Rashid quickly whipped around and responded. "She's good. Mind ya business my nigga," he said, pulling up his khaki pants and exposing his butter colored Timberland boots.

"She is my business. She here with me," Naseef replied coolly. He had reached us on Germantown Avenue, but didn't get too close. The look on his face was one I hadn't seen before. This face was sinister; he was itching to pop off.

"Well this my daughter mother and she taking her ass home," Rashid responded, matching Naseef's ice cold stare.

To end the dispute, I decided to just leave; Rashid wasn't going to make it easy to do shit else. "It's cool Naseef. I'm good. I'll hit you later. I'ma just leave." I shook my head in frustration.

Staring at me with intensity he said, "Aight cool. Make sure you call." He shot Rashid a look and then hesitantly walked up the street, back towards Erie Avenue. Quickly turning away from Rashid in disgust, I walked the twenty feet up the street to my car. Of course he was hot on my trail.

"Goddamn, what you want to carry me to the car Hercules?" I spat, mocking his idiotic and jealous behavior.

"Na I don't wanna carry ya big ass, I just want to make sure you get in ya dirty ass Mustang and carry ya stank ass home," he said trying to be funny. He could laugh all he wanted but I had really just saved his ass. He was out in the hood acting all love-struck, when in reality he was practically by himself. Naseef on the other hand, was down there with four niggas and would have chewed Rashid's ass up out there.

"Stank? Yeah okay, but you out here acting like a nut ass nigga over it." I smacked my

teeth in disgust and kept walking

"Yep. Now get the fuck outta here," he said without shame, as I plopped down in my seat. Slamming the door I was done listening to his stupid ass. Turning the key, the engine roared to life, and I peeled off down the block nearly clipping Rashid with my rearview mirror.

An hour later I lay back relaxing on my suede, European chaise lounge that sat across from my bed. The Grey Goose I had at The Eagle's Bar had set in, and I sat peacefully trying to forget the events from earlier. Although I was slightly inebriated by the time I arrived home, I was sober enough to see that Rashid had followed me home. Of course his ass couldn't get through the gate, so I wasn't worried about him bringing the drama. The nigga was stupid. He had definitely been drinking, and that's the only reason I could fathom he would act the way he did. Bringing a bottle of water to my lips to hydrate my dry throat, I heard my buzzer ring. It was security from the gate calling up. They usually called for one thing; permission for a visitor to come in. *I know Rashid ass ain't coming over here to start some shit. He can miss me with that. His aint coming up in here,* I thought.

"Helloooo," I said, speaking into the receiver that was right by the front door.

"Good evening, Ms. Washington. I'm sorry to disturb you but you have a visitor by the name of Naseef Brown. Should we let him up," the Caucasian sounding security guard asked.

Naseef? What the fuck is he doing here, and how the fuck did he find out where I lived. I guess Rashid ass wasn't the only one that was following me.

"Ummm, yeah sure, let him up," I reluctantly replied. Had Layla been home he would have been sent on his way. I made a mental note to check him about coming to my home unannounced, and about following a bitch on some stalker shit. I ran to the bathroom and quickly brushed some lip gloss on my full lips.

I had just grabbed my bottle of Jadore

perfume and sprayed the top and bottom of my body before I heard the knock at my door. Taking my time, I walked through my apartment and finally opened the door to see Naseef's handsome face.

"Hey," he said, hesitantly. He had made a bold move by showing up to my house, and his face displayed his nervousness.

"Wassup," I asked with a light smile. I was still standing in the doorway.

"Can I come in?" he asked.

"Yea, but I'm going to be going to bed soon. Wassup?" I asked, while reluctantly opening the door and allowing him entrance into my home.

"I came by to check on you. Bull was pretty heated. Just wanted to make sure you was straight," he confessed.

"Well that's nice of you Naseef. I appreciate you checking on me but I don't usually have much company, and it's kind of creepy you followed me," I said. I wasn't tryin to be ignorant since I liked Naseef, but I didn't want anyone following me.

"Well my bad baby. I just wanted to make

sure you was straight. I shoulda called. So that's your babyfather?" he asked, casually dismissing his stalkerish behavior.

"Yeah," I said with a smirk.

"Don't look like ol'boy over you. Or maybe I missed something," he said probing for more information.

Rolling my eyes for the tenth time tonight, I responded, "That's a whole notha issue by itself."

"I got time," he said. I guess I did owe him a little bit of an explanation since it must've been extremely uncomfortable for him.

"Well....First of all, I apologize for that. I didn't mean to put you, or potentially put you in any type of situation. My daughter's father is a jealous type. He wants us to be a family, but he did a lot of shit in the past. We still love each other, but I ain't trying to go there with him. Guess he's not understanding that."

"Soooo basically, you fuckin him, he in his feelings, and you still trying to do you," he said, raising that infamous eyebrow. I guess he was trying to make sense of the situation and sum it up in "nigga" terms.

"That's an inappropriate analysis especially since you aren't my man," I said.

"I could be," he replied. "But the shit that went down earlier, I ain't having. You gotta make sure you and that nigga got an understanding."

"Well me and you aint at that stage so you thinking too far in advance. Besides, I know how to handle my business," I said. As soon as I said that, I regretted my slick choice of words.

"Oh yeah?" he asked, boldly moving toward me. I guess his nervousness had went out the window. I backed into the door since we were still standing in the foyer talking.

"Handle it then," he said now right in front of me, staring me down.

Pressing his body against mine, I was now pinned up against the front door. My breathing grew heavy once I felt the the bulge in his pants pressing against my thigh. Naseef leaned in and kissed my neck. His breathing was raspy and I could smell the alcohol on his breath.

"Damn you sexy as shit, and I could fuck the shit out of you right now. You gon give it to me?" he asked, whispering into my ear. "I just want to taste it."

Ummm. I turned my head and shuddered. His words had me weak. How the hell could I resist him? Those lips would be perfect for sucking on my kitty cat.

I led him to my bedroom and seductively sat back on my chaise lounge. I undid the satin robe I had on so Naseef could see my thick, naked body. I seductively spread my legs to reveal my neatly shaven pussy. Licking my lips at Naseef, I invited him to play. *After all, he did say he wanted a taste right.* It was funny how I could go from zero to ninety when it came to sex. Deep down I was a freak.

Naseef wasted no time coming out of his Timberlands, jeans and t-shirt. He stood in front of me looking like a Thug God. That was until he came out of his boxers...When I say Naseef's dick was about six inches hard, that was pushing it. He wasn't long at all, however it was kind of fat. I ignored the fact that his dick was king of small, and figured what he lacked in length, he made up for with skill...I was wrong.

Naseef's head was good but his cock was straight trash. I wanted to curse him out when he was on top of me huffing and moaning, throwing weak ass strokes.

Me being me, I hopped on top to do me, but that backfired. His ass wasn't prepared for me bouncing my big ass up and down on the dick. He came in less than a minute and the look on my face confirmed to him I wasn't pleased.

To save face, he ate my pussy until I shuddered to make up for his weak performance. He looked good and the nigga had hella swag, but the dick might've been a deal breaker.

FIVE

"I HAD SOOO much fun mommy. We did our nails and put colored hair pieces in each other's hair," Layla exclaimed excitedly. She was telling me about her awesome night at the sleepover. She turned to the side and showed me the pink clip-on hair extension snapped in her straight hair. It was actually pretty cute.

I had just picked her up from the daycare and we were headed home. The daycare gave us until 10 am to pick up the girls, since they knew a lot of single parents would use the girl's night out for themselves as well. I told Naseef he had to leave at eight, much to his dismay. He was sprawled out, comfortable as hell, and was acting like he didn't want to go.

"Well, I'm glad you had fun babe. They gotta do that again sometime soon," I admitted.

"Yesss they do. I like being around the other girls…So are you taking me to my dads'?" Layla asked. I was praying she didn't ask me that. Damn, why couldn't she just hang out with me? I didn't feel like dealing with Rashid and his mouth.

"Umm yeah. I can. I didn't know if you wanted to hang out with me though." I said, pretending to pout.

"Mom, I told you I wanted to go to my dad's. How about this, I give you next Saturday okay," she said, offering the proposal, and touching my arm to make sure I was okay with it. I laughed at my daughter and her display of affection and compromise.

"Okay, deal. I'll text your dad and let him know I'll drop you off." Turning the corner, I changed my course and headed to Rashid's.

◇◇◇

My head was throbbing from last night, so I reached in my purse and shook out an Aleve from a bottle I had. I had just parked my car, and was waiting for Layla to get her things. On my way into the building I saw Rashid's Cadillac parked on the side. For some reason it looked odd; sort of like it was leaning. Rashid was at the door since Layla had called him as we were pulling up. After giving her a quick kiss goodbye I tried to rush off before Rashid could say a word to me, however that move didn't work at all.

"Yo, let me holla at you real quick Nina," he said, as I tried to walk off. I turned around with an attitude.

"Wassup? I asked, looking down at my watch to appear as if I had somewhere to be.

"Come in real quick. We can talk in private and not in the halls."

I reluctantly agreed and went in. Rashid closed the door when we got in his room. I sat down on the edge of the bed while he leaned against the wall before speaking.

"So what's up Nina?" he asked, staring at

me.

"What you mean?" I asked, smiling, again faking innocence.

"Wassup with you, wassup with life…us."

Not again with this shit, I thought. "What were you doing wit Bull…and why you playing games?"

"I'm not playing games, I'm just living my life. And the nigga you saw me with was a friend." I said matching his stare. At the end of the day I was grown. I could admit to what I was doing, but I wasn't going into extra details. It was none of his business.

"Nina….you're playing games…Listen I'ma keep it real with you, and this ain't on no drunk shit cuz I haven't drank shit today. I want us to be a family again. This shit is really getting to me. I want to spend more time with Layla, and I can't really handle seeing you with anyone else. I done cut off the hoes I was fucking wit a long time ago. So why you tryin to play a nigga on some get back shit, when you know that's not what you really want."

What he was saying wasn't far from the truth. We were fucking all the time, and somewhere in my wildest dream we would get back together and live happily ever after. Unfortunately, I had suppressed those dreams a long time ago when he was in and out of jail, and running around with this hoe and that hoe.

I exhaled deeply before speaking. "Rashid…I gave you so many opportunities to do right by me and Layla. So many. You were in an out of jail while I was struggling with your daughter, and when you were home you provided, but didn't give us your time because you were too busy laid up entertaining hoes. Regardless of how different you are now, what the fuck makes you feel that you deserve anything else more from me. It was me, who dealt with hoes getting out of line. It was me, who was going back and forth to court, with no car, in the cold, pushing Layla in a stroller. It was me, who cried damn near every week, not you. So you can miss me with that shit. Why do I fuck you?...hmmm, let me think, because it's good, and convenient.

I was beyond frustrated and so was he. He paused before responding.

"Nina, you gotta remember I was twenty four years old. I was living a fast life and it was fast girls. You always had my heart. A nigga just made mistakes." As soon as he said that, I immediately frowned up my face. He was beginning to push my buttons.

"Mistakes?" I asked, in disbelief. "If it happens once it's a mistake Rashid. When it happens repeatedly, it's a choice...Fuck ya excuses."

"So, that's how you feel permanently. Soooo, basically I aint never gon be shit?" he asked. I didn't respond. I just sat there with the "whatever" look.

Growing frustrated Rashid broke the silence. "So you think we just gon fuck when you want, and you think you gon run around and fuck with other niggas. Yeah okay. Not happening," he said, looking at me like I had lost my mind. I continued to just stare at him. Of course he kept talking.

"Nina I've been home four years. I stopped dealing dope, found a decent job, and have tried to be a better father to Layla, but you still piss on me. What more do you want? You found out about Kiana and I cut her off. I was fucking her because you wasn't even thinking about fucking with me then. I don't deal with nobody else but you. Let me show you've I've changed. I promise I would be a different man," he said sincerely.

I shook my head before looking up at him and responding, "I can't Rashid. I just don't want to disappoint Layla, and I don't want to get fucked over."

"We don't have to say anything to Layla right away. We can continue the way we've been and work on us in the meantime in between time. We can talk, go places, and hang out. At least try. I promise to give you as long as you want, and if things don't work out, at least I tried. I know I won't disappoint you. I can make you happy Nina. I know I can." Damn, the shit he said was so tempting. Indeed I loved him, and I hated that he was bringing those deep old feelings out of me right now. I was always a sucker for the right words.

"Let me give this shit some thought Rashid," I said, considering what he said. He was right. I loved Rashid, but I had been hurt by him. He had changed a lot, and I always had to remind myself that we had been together in our early twenties; six years had passed. Maybe he had changed.

Satisfied with my answer, Rashid went to say something, but was interrupted by a knock at the front door. I looked at Rashid puzzled since he typically didn't have his homey's come over when Layla was there. What surprised me, is that he appeared baffled as well. However, he didn't move to get the door.

"Get the door Rashid," I said, since the knocks were getting louder and increasing in frequency. Someone wanted his ass to come out. Walking to the door, Rashid sighed as I came behind him. As soon as I came behind him and made my way to the door, I could hear the yelling from behind it.

"Open the fucking door Rashid, I see the bitch car outside!"

I immediately recognized the voice. It was Kiana.

"Are you fucking kidding me?" I asked. "This hoe outta line. Layla is in here, so you best go outside and handle that shit. I don't want her hearing or seeing none of that project bullshit. And then you got the nerve to be talking about us getting back together," I whispered, through clenched teeth.

"Nina this shit aint my fault. That bitch been acting retarded since I cut her ass off. Just chill. Go back in the room with Layla for like five minutes and I'ma handle it." Reluctantly, I agreed, and made my way back to the room to make sure Layla was unaware of the drama that was about to unfold.

Five minutes passed and Rashid hadn't come back in the house. Layla was still watching a movie, so I told her to stay in the room so I could go peek outside. Walking out of the house, I heard screaming. I wasn't ready for the drama that was taking place.

"So how you just gon say fuck us for that bitch?!" Kiana screamed, with her finger jammed in Rashid's face.

"Yo, get the fuck outta here. There was

never an "us." Don't worry about me or anyone else I deal with.--Go the fuck head Kiana!" Rashid yelled, extending his arm to create some distance between them.

A wicked smile formed on my face since the argument confirmed that he had indeed cut her off to attempt to be with me. As quickly as the smile came, it left when Kiana saw me standing near the steps and made her way to me. Rashid grabbed her but that didn't stop her from talking shit.

"What the fuck you smiling for bitch. You won't be smiling when I beat ya ass out here?"

I didn't bother to respond, since Kiana clearly wasn't on my level. After all, she was outside begging a nigga who wanted me, and not her. She continued to talk shit until she saw that it was useless and I wasn't going to entertain her.

"Fuck both yall! You keep chasing behind that stank, stuck-up hoe Rashid!" she said as she snatched away from him, and walked back to her car. "I'll bet ya ass will be running right back to me. That's why the both of you motherfuckers will be walking today!" she yelled, while hanging halfway out her older model Ford Crown Victoria.

When she made the comment it rolled over my head, until I glanced over at Rashid's car. The reason it looked odd earlier is because all the tires were flat. Looking over to my car I noticed that my tires were flat as well. *Oh hell no!* Dashing away from the spot I had been watching them from, I went over to my car to confirm that my tires were indeed flat. My eyes confirmed the damage, and I raced to Kiana's Crown Victoria to smack fire out her ass. Not surprisingly, her hood ass didn't flinch. She had come for a fight, and that's exactly what that hoe was about to get.

Coming from behind the car door, Kiana quickly formed a fighter's stance. I on the other hand didn't have time for that stance shit, and swung a hard, right hook. I had no tolerance for drama from hood bitches like her. As soon as I threw the punch, I grabbed her hair and pulled her head down so I could pummel her ass. However, Kiana cleverly used her foot to kick my leg from under me. Ghetto bitches like her were used to having tricks up their sleeves to win fights. I should've known better.

Losing my balance, I fell to the ground, immediately scraping my back on the ground. I still had Kiana's hair tightly gripped in my fist, but she still was leaning over me punching wildly. Even though she could barely see, her punches were still connecting with my face and body. I weakly punched with my free hand but she was too strong, so I took my right foot and kicked her with all my might. Kiana flew backwards and that gave me three seconds to get the hell up or get my ass whooped.

Like The Incredible Hulk, her ass immediately hopped up and charged at me. This time I used her tactic; I threw a punch and tripped her at the same time. She fell to the ground, and I immediately hopped on top of her to sit on her ass so she couldn't move. While she thrashed around wildly and kicked to try to get me off of her, I gripped her cheap hair and began punching her hard in the face.

I had hit her about two or three times before Rashid came and grabbed me off of her. Luckily, a nosey neighbor had called the police when Kiana and Rashid were arguing. Since the neighbor saw Kiana flatten my tires during the argument, she was arrested for vandalism, and Rashid was forced to file a restraining order against her. He was hood but he wasn't stupid. Hoes like her would end up forcing a nigga to smack them. When that happened, the first person they want to lock up is the male. The restraining order would establish the fact that she was the aggressor, and that he wanted to avoid contact with her.

After all the drama, we decided that it would be best if Layla came home. Since Layla really didn't know what was going on, I suggested that the two of them spend the rest of their Saturday night at my apartment. There was no reason to ruin Layla's day with her father because of someone else's bullshit.

After calling AAA and getting the cars towed to repair facilities, we caught a cab back to Willow Grove. I was still a little pissed at Rashid, but hid it since my ass wasn't squeaky clean either.

The rest of the day went very well. I got ahead at work by finishing up some claims, and also managed to do my cleaning and laundry. Around five I made dinner which consisted of meatloaf, mashed potatoes and asparagus. I even threw in some chewy, fudge brownies. The remainder of the night was movies, and Layla taking turns snuggling up on me and Rashid.

The time for us was very relaxing; I didn't even drink one sip that night. Layla also seemed very happy and it was something I could actually see myself doing more; something that I actually was happy to embrace.

I looked over at Rashid and told myself if he did what he said, then we could make it work. As long as he gave at least fifty percent, like I did in every relationship. I wasn't doing any more of that eighty-twenty shit. However, before I could give my fifty percent, I had a small situation to take care of. A small problem called *Naseef*.

Naseef had been calling me almost every damn hour. He didn't want anything. He was carrying the situation like we were a couple and he was checking in. It was becoming annoying since I had other plans for our little "situation". It also didn't help that every time my phone even so much as chirped, Rashid was giving me looks. I definitely needed to handle my situations fast, and figure out what I wanted to do for sure.

SIX

I HANDED THE two crisp dollar bills to the cashier and quickly accepted my change. Throwing it down into an empty cup holder, I reached back out the window and eagerly took my medium Iced Coffee. I took a long sip and smiled; it was sweet just the way I liked it. The sugary, caffeinated drink was just what I needed to get me through the day.

I had just picked up my car from Mr. Tire's to repair the damage from dumb ass Kiana. Two tires had cost me over $200, so I was not in the greatest of moods. Best believe I would be seeing that hoe in court. Call me petty; I didn't give a damn.

Once a month on a Monday, I took off of work and conducted a visual inspection of my properties. This was just to make sure that the halls weren't littered with trash, and that everything was in working order. Today was one of those days. Unfortunately for me, the day wasn't going so smoothly. One of my places had trash and broken beer bottles all over the front, while another had a cat running rampant through it.

After picking up disgusting ass trash and swatting the cat with a stick, I was irritated and tired. I made a note to mail out a memo about the trash, and not leaving the doors open to allow strays to get in. I would raise the rent if the trash continued to be an issue, especially since I was the one who had to foot the bill when the city fined me for it.

Pulling up to my favorite restaurant, Vivienne's Kitchen, I hopped out and ran in to get my crab cake sandwich. Lunch had long passed, and I was more than aware, because of the pains and sounds coming from my stomach. I got back in the car and heard the familiar ding of my phone. I had over a dozen messages a piece from Rashid and Naseef from the course of the day. I was growing irritated since I was busy, and it was only 2pm. I still had to check on the work on my rehab, drive back to Willow Grove to pick up Layla early from her after school program, and meet the babysitter at the house, so I could make it to the bank in time to deposit rent money orders I had picked up from my P.O Box.

The rest of the day went according to plan, although it was still very hectic. I made it to the bank just in time, and headed to the liquor store afterward; I needed a drink. It was around six o clock and starting to get dark when I sat in the car with my bottle of Absolut. I texted the babysitter to make sure that Layla had eaten and done her homework. Rashid had been texting me about coming by his home, but I had other things to deal with at the moment.

Since the babysitter was there, I planned to meet up with Naseef and let him know I wouldn't be seeing him anymore. I could have taken the cowardly route by changing my number, but that possibly wouldn't work since he now knew where I lived. The only thing I could do was be honest and cease the game playing. He was fine, but the dick was trash, and I didn't look at him like husband potential.

Dropping my bottle in the passenger seat, I pulled away from the liquor store and made my way over to see Naseef. I would drink later since I wanted to be sober while dealing with him.

"Hey boo," I said to Naseef, while walking through the door of his condo. It was small, but undeniably beautiful, in a small suburban area outside of Philadelphia called Bala Cynwyd.

"Wassup sexy. You want something to drink?" he asked, before giving me a moist kiss on the lips and leading the way into the kitchen. Of course, that too was small, but was breathtaking with stainless steel appliances and granite countertops. As I quickly scanned the home, I concluded that Naseef was very neat and liked modern fixtures.

Taking the glass he gave me, I went into the living room and sat down on his black leather couch. There were no personal pictures, just artwork and a very large flat-screen television. Joining me in the living room, Naseef took a gulp from his identical cup and stared at me with a smile.

"So wassup with you? What did you want to talk to me about?" he asked. He stared at me intently with slight adoration. I could tell he was clearly smitten with me.

I took a deep breath since it was a little hard for me to cut him off. I liked Nassef, and I knew he was feeling me too. He always wanted to spend time with me, and was very persistent even though I always had an excuse.

"Well Naseef, I'ma just be straight up with you. I like you but I'ma have to chill with seeing and talking to you. Me and my daughter's father…." My voice trailed off when I saw his face change. It now displayed a mixture of irritation and anger.

"You and ya baby father gon get back together," he asked, finishing my sentence.

I nodded my head for confirmation. He just stared at me. "Look Naseef. At the end of the day I do still care about him, and I'm trying to do what I gotta do for my daughter. I don't want to spin you, so I'm just trying to be honest with you. You are good peoples so we definitely can remain friends."

"Friends?" Naseef asked with a smirk, while pausing. "You on some other shit Nina. One minute you acting like you single, and ignoring his calls and texts. You're a game player, but I can dig through the bullshit. I be seeing you on ya phone all the time when you with me…" He paused again for emphasis. "So all of a sudden y'all getting back together but we just fucked last week. I guess you fucked him too right." He sat back on the leather sofa and stared at me intensely, waiting for a response.

I smacked my teeth, since the conversation wasn't going the way I wanted it to. I didn't come to argue, in fact, I hated confrontations and disagreements. I just came to let him know what it was; our budding relationship was over.

"That's irrelevant Naseef, and frankly, I didn't come down here to argue," I responded, somewhat offended by what he had just said. Naseef was still staring me directly in my face, so I looked down at my fiddling fingers to avoid eye contact.

Naseef paused for a minute, as if he was in thought and finally responded. "Nina why you want to fuck up something that can be good for both of us?" he asked. "I mean…You told me the story about all the cheating, and lying and shit. What makes you think anything is gon change. You never gonna be happy if you don't step outside of that and take a chance. You could have that wit me."

I didn't respond. He was right in a way, however, he didn't know Rashid, so he would never see the change I had saw.

"Yo, look at me Nina. Matter fact, come here…come here," he said, motioning with his hand for me to come to him. I stood up and walked in front of him. He took my hands and looked me in the eye.

"Nina give me a chance. I mean…You gon make your own decision, but don't shut me out. In my opinion he won't live up to the promises he done put in your ear, and then you gon be disappointed wishing you had made a different choice. Just don't shut me out," he pleaded. Damn...I was always a sucker for the right words. My situation would never change if I didn't get my weak ass together.

"Okay Naseef," I responded. What I said to him went against everything I stood for, as well as my internal voice that said *don't do it*. It was done though; I had agreed.

After a couple of drinks and more sweet words from Naseef, I found myself sprawled out on his queen size bed getting my pussy devoured. I made sure to cum during that time, just in case the sex was the same as before. Luckily for me, I did. After another lame fuck, I found myself in a peaceful slumber. However, the peace would be short lived.

SEVEN

I WOKE UP abruptly from the blaring sound of my phone going off. The ring was piercing and had also woken up Naseef, who was slowly stretching after being spooned against me for several hours. I reached over to his nightstand, and grabbed my phone just as the ringing stopped. I wiped sleep out of my eyes to see who it was. It was Aunt Sheena. It was 11pm which was still early to a night owl like myself. However, it was late for Aunt Sheena who was now working the 5am opening shift at McDonalds.

I quickly scanned through my messages

and saw that she texted me. *It's important. Call me ASAP.* I quickly dialed her number to see what was up.

"Hey Aunt Sheena," I asked, as soon as she picked up the phone.

"Nina where are you baby? I need you to meet me at Temple Hospital in the ER." Her voice was shaking.

"What's going on Aunt Sheena?" I asked becoming worried. I pushed myself up and sat up straight in the bed.

"It's Briana...Someone found her. She overdosed."

My aunt's voice trembled with fear. I lost my breath and felt like I was about to pass out the moment she spoke those words. However, my sick feeling was quickly overcome with panic that forced me to move.

"I'm on my way Aunt Sheena." I hung up the phone and quickly jumped out of the bed to get my clothes on.

"What's the matter?" Nascef asked me. I couldn't respond. My mind was focused on one thing and one thing only: my sister. I grabbed my belongings and hurried out of the house.

There was no traffic on City Avenue coming out of Bala Cynwyd so I was able to quickly hop on I76, and take the Broad Street exit to Temple University Hospital.

The drive was like déjà vu all over again. It was the same feeling I felt when I went to Onney's; dread. I prayed this time that my sister would be okay. I don't know what I would do if Briana was dead so I tried to stay positive. I knew one thing; if she was gone I wouldn't be able to live with myself for shutting her out of my life, regardless of what she had done. Something had to change with us, and it had to change quickly.

My heart raced as I threw my car in park in front of the automatic doors that read *EMERGENCY ROOM.* Disregarding the fact that it was a no parking zone, I ran through the doors and was met by my Aunt Sheena, who was standing in the lobby talking to a stern faced, middle-age, white man in a lab coat. As I approached the two of them, I saw his badge and realized he was the doctor. Dr. Vick was his name.

I rushed to my Aunt's side as Dr. Vick spoke. Surprisingly, Rashid was already there. He stood up and came by my side as soon as I walked in. I managed to force a worried smile on my face. I appreciated Rashid being right there for me, but I couldn't help the feeling of guilt that weighed down on me. After all, I had just left from Naseef's house.

"Is she okay?" I asked, looking to the doctor while choking back the sob that was begging to escape. I looked at the doctor, my eyes pleading for confirmation.

Aunt Sheena looked to the doctor and said, "It's okay, that's her sister." The doctor cleared his throat and went on to explain.

"Right now my team is doing the best they can to keep anymore of the drugs from absorbing into her blood stream. We injected her with Naloxone, which reverses the effects of the Opioid, however, she had a lethal amount of Heroin in her system, her blood pressure had dropped tremendously and she was almost in a coma when she arrived. She will definitely need to be closely monitored for the next few hours to make sure the overdose process has been eliminated by the Naloxone. Luckily someone found her when they did. Our goal now is to keep her alive. If we are able to do that, she will need a lot of support as well as some aggressive drug rehabilitation treatment. Judging by the marks on her body and her health condition, this isn't something that occurred over night. There's been some ongoing drug abuse for her, however, the unidentified man she was with showed no signs of long term drug abuse, but he was pronounced dead at the scene." Doctor Vick continued to talk but I heard no sound, all I saw were his lips moving.

After he mentioned that she was with a man, my mind zoned out, I didn't hear anything else he said. I knew it had to be Eric. All I remember was feeling the doctor pat my shoulder gently, and whisper words of encouragement. He then walked off quickly down the long hall. At that moment I became overcome with grief. I felt as if I was going to throw up, so I took a deep breath and forced a dry swallow.

As I buried my face in my hands to sob, I felt Rashid wrap his arms around my body to console me. My cries were muffled against his work-shirt. I shook off the feeling of guilt and focused solely on my grief. I looked over to Aunt Sheena who was now sitting in a waiting chair with her face buried in her hands, weeping.

Tears rolled down my face as I prepared to spend the remainder of the night in Temple Hospital's emergency room. Without bothering to close my eyes, I quietly took my head from Rashid's chest and looked off to say a silent prayer to God. I prayed that he get Briana through this ordeal. She had done some fucked up shit but it wasn't her time. I wondered how she had gotten hooked on Heroin, but then again I was too busy being angry, and drowning my pain with alcohol.

Loosening up his embrace, Rashid motioned for me to sit down. As I went to sit, the sound of my name being called from the entrance of the ER caused me to refocus. *Shit*, I thought to myself when I saw who it was. *Now was definitely not the time.*

I looked over to Naseef who was standing in the doorway, and then looked at Rashid apologetically. *Shit*. His face flashed anger, but was quickly replaced with a more solemn one. I knew he wouldn't make a scene in the hospital, especially since we were there for an important matter. Walking away from Rashid, I slowly walked over to deal with Naseef. *The following me around shit was getting on my last nerve.*

"You okay?" Naseef asked, looking into my eyes with a serious expression plastered on his handsome face. He used his right hand to wipe at a dry tear on my face.

"I'm okay. They found my sister…She overdosed. She's on machines right now, but I don't really know how it's gonna go," I said, with more tears quickly forming and spilling over my eye lids.

"Damn," was all he could say. "Well you

know I'm here for you baby. Any time you want to talk; anytime you want to come by or meet up, I'm here," he offered, rubbing my shoulder. He looked like he wanted to hug me. I knew why he didn't; Rashid was probably staring a hole into my damn back.

"Thank you," was all I managed to muster up. My mind was still bogged down with "what if" thoughts about Briana.

"Well look, I'ma go. I'll text you. I see ya baby-father over there mugging. I know I shouldn't be here. Stay strong Nina…I'll call you okay," he whispered before he walked out. I stood there for a minute and then turned around to go sit down. Rashid was now seated and staring out the window while Aunt Sheena was pacing the floor of the cold waiting room. I sat down in the green floral chair beside Rashid. Surprisingly, he took my hand into his. I knew that was just the calm before the storm. I said nothing since the most important matter was Briana.

My mind swirled with thoughts that had me jittery. I called the babysitter to let her know I would be in very late. She was scheduled to stay overnight in the guest room anyway, so I was merely checking in with her. Layla was already in bed, since by now it was well after midnight. Eventually the events from the night began to catch up with me, and I found myself heavy with fatigue. I closed my eyes and rested my head on Rashid's shoulder. A couple hours later I was awakened by the sound of Dr. Vick. We all stood up quickly to hear the news.

"She's weak but she's going to be alright. We've stabilized her and she's resting, but you all can go in and see her one at a time. We'll probably keep her a few more days until she gets her strength back, but she will be absolutely fine. She's definitely going to need drug treatment…Does she have health insurance?" he asked.

"No, but that's not an issue. You all can send me the bills and I'll see to it she gets the help she needs. I just need some recommendations," I quickly responded. Money would not be a concern as far as getting Briana the help she desperately needed.

Just because I didn't trust my sister, didn't

mean I didn't love her. Maybe this was a sign from God. One thing I was sure about was that my sister needed support, and this drug addiction was likely the cause of her larcenous behavior. I was praying that we could get her some help and she would go back to being the Briana we all knew and loved.

After signing a bunch of papers and giving the hospital my credit card information, we all went back to peek on Briana. She was still asleep, and had an IV hooked up to her arm. Her beauty remained intact, but I could still immediately tell that there was drug abuse. She had lost quite a bit of weight on her already petite frame. Her skin appeared dull, and her hair was pulled back in a dry bun. Tears immediately began to reform and cascade down my face. Seeing her in that state was not easy. We didn't stay much longer, since it was clear she needed her rest.

Aunt Sheena and I gave Briana a kiss goodbye and then the three of us headed out. I knew this was nobody's doing but Eric, and as soon as she woke up and was strong, I would get to the bottom of what was going on in her life.

"Why was the nigga up at the hospital Nina?" Rashid asked. I knew he was going to bring up the dreaded discussion, after all it was only right. Despite him being entitled to ask the question, I was still highly irritated. My sister was in a hospital bed and he insisted on coming to my house instead of his, to question me about a nigga.

"He was just there for support Rashid," I said, trying to quickly get off the subject. I wasn't ready for a slew of questions, and I wasn't in the right mindset to be trying to make up lies.

"Support? Yeah okay… You're lying Nina. I couldn't reach you all night and he just pop up to the hospital for support...Sounds like you were with the nigga before you got there, and you didn't expect me to be there... Why didn't you call me when you found out? Your Aunt Sheena called me when she couldn't get ahold of you. That's the only reason I knew about

Briana. Answer those questions Nina," he demanded, before pausing and waiting for a response. I didn't know what to say so I decided to tell the truth, sort of.

"Look Rashid. I was with him before, but that was only to tell him I was done with seeing him. I had a long day, I lost track of time, and I had a couple of drinks…"

"You fuck that nigga?" he asked, cutting me off.

"No," I lied. I avoided eye contact with him so he couldn't detect the deceit that was written all over my face.

"Listen to me Nina, and hear me when I say this… Don't play games with me. That's not what you want. I didn't come into this situation with the same mindset as before. I'm keeping shit real with you, and I expect you to do the same with me. I don't want to find out you lying to me and that you hiding something…Cuz if you are…" He didn't finish. He didn't need to, because I already knew what he was trying to say. Plus the mean ass look on his face pretty much summed it up.

"I understand Rashid," I said, before he

walked out. I guess he came over just to tell me that. I didn't really like to see Rashid riled up like that. It was very uncomfortable for both of us. My momma always told me emotions weren't to be played with since everyone didn't always know how to control them.

Clearly I had made a mess that I needed to clean up, and clean up fast.

EIGHT

THE NEXT DAY I woke up bright and early despite being up until the wee hours of the morning. After paying my babysitter Ms. Barbara, I tried to conduct business as best as I could. I had informed my manager at work about my family emergency, and he agreed to work with me to the best of his ability. I would still be doing my paperwork as normal, but my availability would be limited to emails and instant messages.

As I headed down to North Philly to pick up my Aunt Sheena, my phone chirped for the tenth time. Naseef had been texting me non-stop, while Rashid had fell back with communicating for the day. He hadn't even called me with his "hey baby, good morning" routine he'd been doing since we started back seeing each other. He was still pissed off and frankly, I couldn't blame him.

I didn't bother to even look at the messages since by the end of the day, Naseef was going to be blocked. You see, I was a business woman and I wasn't going to change my number and disrupt my business, so I was going to block his pesky ass. That way, no texts, calls, or voicemails would come through from Naseef. I hated to do that but at the end of the day, I wasn't a hoe and I wasn't going to keep going between two men. I wanted to try to attempt a relationship with Rashid, and it wasn't possible with Naseef bugging every hour and complicating things. I didn't give a damn how sexy his ass was.

I wasn't about that life in a sense. I knew it was going to be a mess since my behavior today definitely contradicted my actions and words from yesterday. What a web I had spun.

I pulled up to my building in North Philly

and called Aunt Sheena to let her know I was outside. I was picking her up so we could go to Temple to see Briana. After two minutes, she walked out wearing a purple sundress with her hair braided into a bun. It was the beginning of fall, but it was still warm enough outside to wear a dress without a jacket. She looked very nice.

"Hey Aunt Sheena," I said, forcing a bright smile, despite the circumstances.

"Hey Nina." For some reason she looked a little worried, like something was on her mind.

"You okay?" I asked.

"I'm fine, but I do need to talk to you about something," she said, adjusting her body in the seat, and pulling down the seatbelt to secure herself.

"Okay…" I said, puzzled.

"Stop by McDonalds though, I wanna get a coffee, and then we can park up and talk."

"Okay."

I nervously drove up a few blocks and quickly found a McDonalds. They were plentiful in North Philly, so it didn't take long at all. After ordering Aunt Sheena's coffee, and a strawberry banana smoothie for myself, I parked in the parking lot so we could discuss whatever she had in mind.

"Wassup, Aunt Sheena?" I was a little nervous because I wasn't sure what she had to tell me. Whatever it was, she surely had sprang it on me at the last minute, and it seemed important to her judging by her hesitation. My heart skipped a little as she began to talk. She took a deep breath and spoke.

"Well, hopefully this isn't too much on you at once, but I wanted to do the right thing since it's been burning a hole in me for quite some time now." I raised my eyebrow in curiosity. She had my full attention.

"The doctor called and said Briana is up and doing a whole lot better today. Days before they found her, I told her exactly what I'm about to tell you…Your mom was very good to me…" she said, pausing. I had no idea where Aunt Sheena was going with this conversation, but I decided to just listen and not interrupt.

"She was a lot like you. She had a good heart. She had big dreams. She took very good care of her kids... I was a lot like Briana. I was loving but self-centered. And wooooooo", she said, shaking her head for emphasis, "when I got on drugs, the loving part just left with the rest of me. Your father and your mother were together as teenagers. He was killed when you were still a toddler. Your mother never got over that and struggled with depression...With two children to raise by herself she fell deeper into darkness. She still worked and took care of you all with our mothers help... Eventually, our mother got sick and a year later, she passed. That's when things took a turn for the worse. She got strung out on drugs really bad. She had started using during her depression, but she still was functioning. I never said a word. I never warned her about what crack would do to you. I didn't care. I was jealous of your mother. She was everything I wanted to be. I watched her drug herself away, even after what she had done for me..."

"I don't mean to cut you off Aunt Sheena, but I'm confused," I stammered, hating to interrupt. "What had she done for you that has you feeling so guilty now, and why did you say my mother was raising two kids after my dad died. I thought we all had the same father. So Briana has a different dad?" I asked, rambling question after question in an attempt to make sense out what she was saying.

"Yes, she does…She has a different father because…Briana's my child Nina…Not your mothers… She's my daughter…," she said looking away and out the window. What she just said had my mouth wide open. Anything could have flew in it.

"What? Briana is not my sister?" I asked, stunned.

"No. She's your cousin. Your mother raised her until she passed away."

"Why?" I asked, still confused. I had no inclination that Briana wasn't my real sister, and I was truly blown away by the revelation.

"I was so badly strung out Nina… When Briana was six months old, I went on a week-long crack binge. I was in and out of the house with a bunch of random men and women. Briana was there alone half the time. Your mother was calling me, and not getting an answer. So she decided to just pop up at my house to check up on me. When she came by the door was unlocked, and I was passed out with a man in the living room while Briana was in the back room on the floor screaming. She had fallen and she was hungry. She hadn't eaten, and she was soiled up her back. I saw her, I heard her, but the crack consumed me...That day, your mother took her. She said as long as Briana had family in this world, she would be loved. And that's what she did. She loved Briana like her own. This was before she got on drugs. When she got on drugs I didn't think about all that she had done for me. I didn't think about you girls. I just thought about how perfect your mom always seemed and her being on drugs. I looked at it like, she finally showed the world she was no better than me... Gosh I was so fucked up. I was jealous, I was hateful, and I was spiteful. I was just like my child Briana is to you."

I didn't say anything, but it made sense. Briana did always look a little different. She was always lighter and she was way always way smaller. It actually made perfect sense. My mother had never treated her any different from the rest of us, and I had never even heard so much of a whisper about this family secret.

"Wow…" was all I could say. "So you told Briana this?" I asked, feeling deceived.

"Yes. She was shocked but she too said it made sense. Listen Nina, the main thing I want to get at is, Briana isn't well. She's hooked on drugs, and she had a very dysfunctional relationship with Eric. She needs help. She needs rehab and she needs therapy so she can let go of whatever's making her bitter towards you. But here me when I say this, don't let her hatred break you down. I've seen the wear and tear on your spirit since this has happened. You are a wonderful person, but *you* have to see that… I noticed the drinking all the time… I noticed you overwork yourself, and I also noticed the hood ass nigga that was at the hospital. When I called Rashid last night I expected you to be with him. When that guy popped up at the hospital, I realized then, that you were playing with fire."

"I know Aunt Sheena," I said, looking away. She damn sure didn't miss a beat, and I had done my best to hide my struggle within.

"I'm going to take care of that, and I'm gonna also get myself together. I've been feeling guilt when it comes to Briana and I don't understand it. That's why I drink. It helps me cope with everything. I always felt like I did something wrong. Like I failed her somehow. My greed consumed me. Onney lost her life behind my greed...My scheme. I feel like I don't deserve what I have. It's like I want this fairy tale life, and it's in front of me, but I can't accept it because I don't deserve it."

"You can have a good life Nina, and you will have it; you just have to accept it...You can't blame yourself for everything, especially Onney's death. You all were adults. You all made informed choices, and she choose to take her life. She had options, just like you did. You fought under pressure, while she gave up. You can't take the blame for that, and you can't blame yourself for Briana either. You are only responsible for Nina. It took me years to leave that person within me behind. Until she's able to do it, all you can do is support her with distance filtering your love. And Rashid loves you too. I hear it in his voice. I see it in his eyes.

You just have to let him show you with his heart. People change, and I do believe that he has."

"I know…I'll make it right. Everything…I love you Aunt Sheena, and I'm glad you're well and in my life."

"I love you too baby, and so does your sister Briana, deep within her heart. Until she shows it, you focus on the ones around you that are showing it. And you accept it, because you are worthy of it."

The conversation with Aunt Sheena brought a lot of clarity, and had me feeling like a weight had been lifted off of my shoulder. I never really spoke much of my feelings of guilt for Onney's death and Briana's actions. Now thinking about it, I don't know why I would blame myself behind how Briana acted anyway. I guess being her older sibling, *or so I thought*, made me feel like I was responsible for her. No matter what anyone said, I still felt like I failed her.

I found a place to park on a run-down street a few blocks from Temple Hospital after we arrived. I hit my key fob twice to make sure my door was locked, and after stepping around numerous potholes, we arrived at the entrance and made our way up to the fourth floor where Briana was staying. I knew it would be awkward going in there after my aunt's revelation, but I had to talk to Briana, find out what was going on with her, and let her know that I cared.

Walking into the room my emotions were mixed. Bri was sitting on the bed and I didn't know whether to slap her or hug her. I was happy as hell she was alive and well, but I was still angry with her for her betrayal. For now, I wouldn't focus on that. I figured if I could get to the bottom of what was going on with her, then everything would eventually make sense.

"Hey how are you feeling?" I asked, putting down my purse in the visitors chair beside the bed.

"I—I'm okay," she stammered, quickly looking at Aunt Sheena and then back at me.

"So this is your surprise?" Briana asked,

still looking at me, but talking to Aunt Sheena. Aunt Sheena nodded.

"Briana has been asking about you and Layla. She didn't expect you to come up here, but I told her that's not your character. You're love for her outweighs all." She turned to Briana to speak.

"She forgives you Briana,...but she needs answers. We need to know what's going on with you. What made you do the things you did, and how you ended up in here?" I didn't say a word. I just looked at Briana and waited for a response.

"Where do I begin…" she huffed, before her eyes began to water. Aunt Sheena went over and rubbed her back, while Briana lowered her head and nervously tugged on her plastic hospital bracelet.

"Ever since we were young, it's been difficult overcoming the feeling of being unloved…I mean, I knew you loved me, and Onney sometimes, but I always felt like I was missing something…I was always jealous of Nina." She finally looked up at me and began speaking to me directly.

"You were always prettier, had a nicer shape and all the cute guys wanted to talk to you. Hell, I even had a crush on Rashid back in the day before you two got together; back when he used to be on the block," she laughed dryly.

"You were always so strong; so sure of yourself. You had a vision for us, to get us out of poverty and make it. You always got on me about my grades and about the shit I was doing out in the streets. I knew you loved me, but I couldn't help but envy you. I wanted to be just like you... When you got out of community college and got the job at Aetna I became even more jealous. When we started getting big money I tried to step my game up...But it wasn't enough. Here you were, buying properties, getting promoted at Aetna, and about to open a nail salon. I wasn't doing shit. I felt like I could never please you. The money was serious. I wanted to party. I wanted to have fun. I started getting high...Smoking weed. And just as quickly as the money came, it went. I envied you," she repeated. "I wanted your life....And then, I met

Eric... He treated me so good in the beginning. He had me thinking I was his everything, his number one." Her voice cracked at the mere mention of Eric.

"I opened up a little too much. I let him know how much money we were getting. He started asking questions. He played me against you. He talked about how selfish you were, and how you were stacking your money and getting rich while I was fucking mine up. It was all a game to him…" Her voice trailed off as she stared out the window.

"One day when I was drunk, he introduced me to a new drug. He said he did it all the time, but he never said what it was. I found out later that it was Heroin. By then it was too late…And like that, I was broke." She snapped her finger for emphasis. "Well, I was damn near broke anyway. That's when he introduced the idea of blackmailing you. I hated myself…But the drugs took over. It was a struggle just keeping myself up so you wouldn't notice. Over time the signs starting showing, and eventually you found out…But that was just the beginning of my problems.

Even though I did the shit I did, you still gave me my cut of the money. I thought Eric would be happy...He wasn't though. He was furious. He said I was careless. That you never should have discovered our identity. He wanted more. That joint bank account was the worst idea of my life. He took damn near every bit of that money...One day while he was taking a shower, someone called his phone. It was a woman...His wife. Eric was married." Briana paused and choked back a sob. I too was tearing up. My sister had been brainwashed and used.

"She and I started arguing on the phone. I lied and told her I was pregnant. That's when the real truth came out. She started screaming on the phone about how Eric didn't give a shit about me. That he was taking my money and bringing it home to her and their two kids. He had just deposited $100 grand in their account...The worst part was Eric never used heroin. He sold it. He had intentionally gotten me hooked on it to use me...Here I was trying to fit in with him like a fool...Destroying myself...And my family." Briana cried as she shook her head from side to side, before placing them in her hands."

"I felt so betrayed," she continued. "I loved him so much. You were right," she said, looking up at me with a tear stained face. "I hated him and I hated myself...So I loaded up the syringe with a strong cut and poisoned him with the same thing he was poisoning me with. I ended him the same way he had ended me...I wanted him dead, and I wanted to be dead too. Cops really didn't care...They didn't even ask what happened. The just saw two black junkies who had overdosed. One dead and one barely clinging to life," she said, with emptiness.

"Eric wasn't even his government name. That's just what the streets knew him as. It'll take days before his family knows he's gone. I'm not worried though. Many feared him, but very little loved him," Briana added.

The room was silent for a couple of minutes while we let all that Briana had said sink in. *Wow*, was all I could think. Briana had really given Eric a lethal dose of heroin. I guess Karma was a bitch.

I got up, and went over to the bed to give

her a hug. I empathized with all that she had been through, and my heart ached for her, however, the focus now was to get her well. After a couple minutes of saying nothing, I proceeded.

"Listen Briana," I said, finally speaking for the first time since I had gotten in the room. "I forgive you, but I will never forget what you did. I love you and that's why I'm standing here today. If you cross me again, I will write you off for good....You need help, and we want to get it for you. I've already called Valley Forge Treatment Center and they can take you in as early as tomorrow. It's a 30 day inpatient treatment, and it's in Norristown. I figured it would be easy if you were in a different environment...I know 30 days seems like a long time, but your body will need time to get used to being off Heroin. After that, I will pay for all three of us to go to therapy. Clearly, we have some trust and resentment issues we need to work on. If this is okay with you, then I'll go ahead and set everything up. If it's not, then I won't. But I do want to be clear that this is the only way that we can move forward. This is the only way that we can work on having any type of relationship ever again," I said sincerely. The ultimatum had been given. I waited patiently for her to respond.

"Okay," she said. "I want us to be a family again," she replied, quietly.

So it was settled. I arranged to pick Briana up the next day in the afternoon when she was discharged. I was praying that rehab would be enough to get her on the right track. I knew it would be a long road and this was only the beginning.

NINE

On the ride home I felt a sense of calm. I would finally be getting my baby sister back. Sister, cousin, whatever you wanted to call it. She was still my sister to me. With things on track and arranged for Bri, I decided it was time to refocus my energy on my home.

Layla had been seeing Ms. Barbara more than her own mother, and Rashid and I were barely speaking. I was ready to make things right, and bring peace to my life. I had already blocked Naseef since he continued to call non-stop like a deranged person. I was starting to think that Naseef wasn't wrapped too tight. He exhibited such weird behavior. He was clingy, obsessive, and very persistent, which was a sharp contrast from the self-assured and confident attitude he displayed.

I peeked at the clock on my stereo and realized it was lunch time, so I figured I'd catch Rashid while he was on his lunch break at work.

While still focused on the road, I reached into my oversized purse to grab my phone. After voice dialing Rashid, I waited for him to answer.

"Hello," he answered in a distorted voice. He sounded like he had a mouthful of food.

"Hey Rashid…How are you?" I asked, hoping he was in a better mood today.

"I'm good. How'd everything go at the hospital today? I know you said you were going back up there," he said, while chomping and swallowing on the last of whatever he was eating.

"Everything went well. Briana agreed to go to a drug treatment program I found, so I'll be taking her over there tomorrow to get her admitted… So much has happened today. I'll tell you all about it later. I was hoping you were coming by tonight. I'm going to make some lasagna and spend some time with Layla. It's gonna be quiet for the most part."

"Yeah, I'll be by after I get off. I need you to wash my uniform for me though. I ain't gon feel like driving all the way home tonight and getting up at 5."

"I gotchu boo," I said before saying bye and hanging up the phone. I was so happy he was in a better mood. Rashid was one of those people that didn't dwell on things. He addressed it, and that was that.

Before driving off, I returned a few emails from my phone, and afterwards, began my journey back to Willow Grove. First I had to stop to the market and get the ingredients for tonight's dinner.

Rashid walked in around six in the evening. There had been an accident on the expressway, so he was a little later than I had anticipated. As usual, he was tired, so I told him to go relax and I would have dinner ready soon.

After piling on a final generous layer of cheeses, I shoved the pan of lasagna in the oven. My five cheese lasagna was the bomb, and I couldn't wait to dig into it. I peeked in the living room at Layla and Rashid only to see that they were curled up watching the Disney show, *Austin and Ali*. *I really could get used to this*, I thought. They looked so beautiful together, and it wasn't nothing like coming home to a house filled with love.

Rashid had truly grown up. He wasn't out running the streets anymore, he was working, and he was saving his money. He wanted *us* to work out. The ball was in my court, and I was gonna make it work.

An hour and a half later, everyone had eaten and fatigue was setting in. I sent Layla to bathe, and I began loading up the dishes in the dishwasher.

"Rashid, you know where everything is, so you can go and get ready for bed if you want. I know you gotta be up early to get to work on time. You have some boxers here from before. I'll wash your uniform for you. Just leave it out," I yelled into the living room, while simultaneously scraping food away from the plate I was holding.

"Aight, cool. Where you want me to sleep?" he asked.

"Where else?" I replied, with a mischievous grin.

Smiling back, he replied, "I can get used to this for sure."

TEN

I PULLED ONTO the side block of the hospital I had grown accustomed to parking on during Briana's short stay at Temple. Before getting out, I checked my emails, and made a mental note to reply later.

I had just dropped Layla off at school, and I was still a little tired from the night before. Rubbing my eyes, I stared into the mirror, and confirmed that I still looked presentable despite how I felt. I slathered on another coat of clear lip-gloss on my plump lips, and got out of the car to walk up to the hospital.

Today was the big day. Briana was being

released around noon, and I was going to take her to lunch before driving her over to Norristown to the rehab facility. I was excited. It had been months since our falling out, and I was eager to move on from all the negativity and drama.

Walking up to the hospital, I was oblivious to the fact that someone was walking up behind me, until I heard my name being called.

"Nina hold up," a familiar voice called to me. As I went to turn around I felt a strong hand grab my arm. Pulling away, I spun around and saw Naseef.

"Uhh, hey. Wassup," I asked hesitantly. I took a deep breath. He didn't look very friendly, so I wanted to limit the conversation.

"Wassup with you stranger? You ignoring me and shit," he said. I was no longer walking, instead, I was standing on the curb not too far from the hospital.

"Look Naseef, I have a lot going on right now. I'm just focused on getting things right with me and—"

"You and who? Ya fucking babyfather," he asked, cutting me off. I smacked my teeth, and turned around to walk away. I didn't have time for the bullshit.

"Bitch, I'm talking to you, where the fuck you going?" he asked, while grabbing my arm again to stop me. I turned around and looked at him like he had lost his mind. This man before me, I didn't recognize. He had done a complete 360.

"Bitch?" I asked, to make sure he hadn't lost his mind. "Naseef don't disrespect me, and definitely don't play yaself. I blocked you because you bug. You and I don't exist. Maybe in another world... You good people, just not right for me. So don't come out her and discredit yaself by acting like a nut."

"So you back with that nigga now. How though? I was just fucking you a couple days ago. We just talked about this shit," he said while getting closer and adjusting his pants. The muscles in his jaws clenched as he spoke confirming his anger. This nigga was buggin, and I wanted no parts of it.

"Look Naseef boo, I'm good. I'm going to try to make things work with my baby father. I apologize for leading you on. We can remain friends but I can't deal with you like that anymore," I said.

"Naaa," he said, while shaking his head. "You foul as shit. You trying to shit on me. I can get any bitch out here…"

"Well go get em Naseef…Fuck you standing here for, beating a dead horse?" I asked. Before I knew it, he had grabbed me by the collar of my jacket and pulled me into him.

"Bitch, I'll make ya fuckin life hell," he said, with a snarl.

I snatched away, and yelled, "Don't put ya fucking hands on me, you fucking nut," I yelled, with wide eyes.

"Bitch you haven't seen a nut. But you will…" He walked off and didn't look back. I stood there staring at his back, as he proceeded down the street, and turned the corner. The nigga had followed me of course.

I had heard the stories, but never had I actually dealt with a fatal attraction type of situation. I mean, I had experienced the jealousy…But this, this was something different. This nigga wasn't wrapped too tight. I could see the look in his eyes. He clearly wasn't taking rejection well. I cursed myself, since this was essentially all my fault. I would tell people what they wanted to hear and then rescind, like they were crazy. The lies and games were catching up to me, and I didn't like it one bit.

I shrugged off the bad vibes I had developed and continued the walk up and into the hospital. I continued up to the fourth floor to Briana's room, where I was greeted with a warm smile.

She looked a lot better sitting on the edge of the bed. She was still thin, but she seemed a lot better in spirit than before.

"Hey Nina," she said, standing up to give me a hug.

"Hey boo," I said, while embracing her. "I see you're ready. Did they give you release papers yet?" I asked. Briana had her little hospital bag neatly packed and placed by the door. Aunt Sheena had brought her something to wear, so she looked nice and put together.

"No not yet. They told me they would have them ready in about an hour." She sat back down on the bed.

"Let me ask you something Briana...Remember the guy Nassef that I met at the book store, Black and Nobel. We were in there together, and you introduced me, saying he was a friend."

"Oh yeah, I remember that day. Naseef is a friend of Eric's brother.

As soon as Briana spoke those words, my stomach churned. I didn't want to fuck around with anyone affiliated with him. Eric was a scumbag potential killer, so I knew the apple didn't fall too far from the tree for Naseef's ass either. *The company you keep...*

"Oh damn, I didn't know that," I said nonchalantly.

"Naseef never came around much. I met him a few times. He was on a different level. He was only a couple years older than Eric, but he had a different vibe about him. He was always quiet, but niggas always seemed to flock to him. He was always with Rodney, Eric's older brother...Remember when Onney died, Rodney was in the car with Eric when he drove us up to her house."

As soon as she said that, a bell went off in

my head. I remembered Rodney! I only glanced at him a couple of times in the car during the ride, but he was with Naseef the night at the Eagles Bar. That's why he kept staring. He remembered me, but I didn't recognize him. It seemed odd that he didn't speak.

"Oh ok, I remember Rodney now," I said, not going into too much detail with Briana.

"Why you ask about Naseef?" Briana asked, curiously.

"No reason. I had went out for drinks with him a few times," I lied.

"Oh well be careful girl. That's if you plan to see him again. I heard that nigga was in the disposal business."

"Disposal business? What the hell is that," I asked naively.

"Eric told me that Naseef is a real killer… He puts anyone to sleep for the right amount of money. I heard he's good at it too. I heard he has a nice ass condo out in the county, along with plenty money tucked in the bank off them bodies."

"Oh wow," I said. Truthfully, that was all I

could really even get out. I was at a loss for words. Naseef was a killer and my black ass had just put this nigga in the worst place; his feelings.

I decided to get off the topic of Naseef. Lately I was getting the shitty end of the stick. I contemplated getting a restraining order. This nigga could easily follow and find me. He knew where I lived, and he flat out said he would make my life hell. I was once again shook. Yeah, that restraining order sounded real good.

After waiting about two hours, the nurse finally showed up with Briana's release papers. She had only been there for three days but it seemed longer. After thanking the staff we said bye and headed to Maggiano's downtown. I figured I would feed her good before she went to the rehab. Lord knows what they would have on their menu, and besides, kicking heroin was no easy task.

In the hospital, Briana was given medication to take away the cravings for the drug, but outside it was a whole different story. She was already getting a little fidgety, and was scratching at her arm periodically.

We walked into Maggiano's Little Italy right before the lunch rush, so luckily we didn't have to wait for a table. The hostess sat us at a small, two person booth, in a quiet corner of the restaurant. Two minutes later, our waitress, a brown haired young man, by the name of Tom, brought us water and proceeded to take our order.

I ordered Shrimp Scampi, while Briana got the Shrimp Fra Diavolo. I glanced at the time and saw it was 11:15 am. I was right on time to have her over in Norristown and checked in before 3. My goal was to get her there early, and get back well before it was time to pick up Layla from her after school program.

We made small talk for twenty minutes until our food arrived. I wasted no time digging into the plate of piping hot scampi. While I ate, my phone began to vibrate repeatedly. I looked down and didn't recognize the number, so I didn't answer it. The vibration stopped and within ten seconds, it began again.

"Why you don't answer that?" Briana

asked, while shoving a forkful of shrimp, and fettuccini in her mouth.

"I don't recognize the number," I said.

Briana laughed and asked, "What you got bill collectors calling or something. Not Big Money Nina." The snide remark caught me off guard, but I remembered what Aunt Sheena said, and dismissed it as pure jealousy. I paid all my bills in full and on time. She knew damn well it wasn't a bill collector.

I grabbed my phone off the wooden booth, and decided to answer it.

"Hello," I said, hesitantly.

"Hey baby," Naseef said, greeting me. He was acting so fucking stupid, like I hadn't just told him to fuck off a couple hours ago. The nut had called me from a different number. Without responding, I immediately hung up the phone.

"Can't stand fucking telemarketers," I lied.

We finished our food a half hour later, and made our way to Norristown. After getting Briana settled in, I prepared for my journey back home. I had the next day off, and I would use that to relax since I would be going back to my regular work schedule the upcoming Monday.

I looked down at my phone for the hundredth time that afternoon. The messages I had received sent chills through my body.

Bitch, you trying to play me, I'll destroy you and that little family of yours. Ask about me.

I didn't need to ask, I already knew. What I didn't understand was how a grown ass man was acting this damn immature. A bitch didn't want you. Move on. I shook my head, still baffled by this whole ordeal. My Aunt Sheena told me I was playing with fire. I wonder if she knew anything else about Naseef. I was damn sure going to ask her.

I was going to wait to tell Rashid about the bullshit Naseef was up to. I loved Rashid, but he wasn't on Naseef's level. I didn't want to get him caught up in the drama. There was no telling what Naseef might do when his feeling were involved.

ELEVEN

It was around nine the next morning when I walked out of the Criminal Justice Center on Filbert Street. I was pissed off to the max.

I had gone in to get a restraining order but was basically dismissed. I was told that I didn't have a justifiable reason to have a restraining order issued. According to them, "I'll make your life hell," wasn't technically a threat. The multiple times he followed me also didn't quite classify as stalking, especially since we had only recently stopped being intimate. Apparently they wanted him to follow me a few more times after we stopped fucking and then it would be deemed stalking. All I could do was roll my eyes, and take deep breaths to keep from going off.

No wonder why bitches were getting killed left and right by deranged lovers. I was definitely at a crossroad. Naseef was still calling. He had actually called several more times after we left the restaurant. Each time he called from a different number. I was starting to think he really didn't even have a job like he said. The nigga had way too much time on his hands.

Just as I was crossing the street to head to my car, my phone ring. This time the number came up as unknown.

"Hellooo?" I asked frustrated. The phone games were getting annoying.

"Nina—don't hang up!" Naseef said, quickly.

"What do you want Naseef? I told you it's over between us. This shit is getting annoying and you coming across as a fuckin nut."

"I know Nina…and I don't know why you got me acting like this. I can't help how I feel about you yo. You lied to me and tried to play me."

"Well, I'm sorry...I really do apologize. What I did was wrong...but please leave me alone," I begged. I looked around cautiously before climbing into the seat of my Mustang. There was no telling where he was at.

"Bitch, it's not over, till I say it's over," he snapped, in a threatening tone.

Pausing into the phone, I responded. "Naseef, I just filed a restraining order against ya ass. This is some stalking shit. A bitch don't want you. Your dick is lame and yo ass is also lame as shit. Grown ass man, on the phone crying over some pussy. I'm back with my babyfather—"

"You think I give a fuck about a fucking restraining order," he spat, cutting me off in midsentence. Apparently none of the other shit I had just told him registered.

"Naseef, you are above this, just go head...please," I whined. I rubbed my temple in frustration.

"No bitch...I'm above you. And I will be above you when I stomp out ya fucking teeth," he threatened. The words he spoke came out cold with venom.

I quickly hung up the phone. I wanted to cry. He said he would make my life hell and that's exactly what he was doing. I was at a crossroads. I had to wait for a restraining order, and Naseef wasn't backing off. I was scared as fuck. My plan was to limit my movement for a little while until he fell back. There was nothing else I could do, and my hands were tied.

Two weeks passed and things were going pretty good. Briana was doing very well in rehab and was two weeks from coming home. She was getting back to her old shallow self again.

The first week had been hell for her because of the heroin withdrawals. She would scream, kick, curse, cry, throw up, and anything else you could imagine from a heroin addict in withdrawal. Watching her in that state was hard, but Aunt Sheena and I did it.

I walked through the secured gates of

Valley Forge Treatment Center and waited to be buzzed in. After showing my id to the security guard and signing in, I walked back to the outside lunch area where Briana was eating at a small table, by the swimming pool

"Hey boo," I said, greeting Briana, who was eating a BLT.

"Hey Nina," she said with a smile, before wiping her hands on a napkin and pushing her sandwich to the side.

"Just came to see how you were doing and talk to you a little bit about something. How's everything going?" I asked.

"It's going good. Ready to get out of here and get back to my house. I know I have a ton of mail in my mailbox."

"Naaa, Aunt Sheena has been stopping by to put your mail up and make sure the neighbor's dog hasn't been shitting in the yard," I laughed. "You know they got into it. The dog had shit all up in ya yard and Aunt Sheena stepped in some. She walked over there and told them to keep that damn dog out the yard. The lady called herself getting smart and Aunt Sheena told her she would woop her ass and smear that dog shit in her face when she was done."

Briana was in tears as I told her the story.

"Naaa, but on some real shit, I wanted to talk to you about something serious," I said, changing the subject.

"Wassup?" Bri asked, curiously.

"Rashid got promoted to training supervisor. His actual training begins in two weeks, and lasts for a month."

"That's wassup girl! Rashid doing his thing. Yall back together," she asked smiling.

"Yeah girl. It's actually going pretty good. We been seeing each other on and off, but for the past few weeks he been at my place--The job is in Baltimore Bri," I said quickly, with a serious look.

"He asked for us to come…Me and Layla…He wants me to wrap up what I have here and get a condo out in Baltimore. By the time he's finished his training we will already be settled in." I waited for her to respond.

When Rashid proposed the idea I didn't hesitate. So much had happened in Philly, and it was time to get away. I had plenty money in the bank, a nice job, and more recently a beautiful, complete family. It also didn't hurt that I would be able to free myself from Naseef's crazy ass.

He had fell back with the phone calls but I still didn't feel safe. I figured moving would be a fresh start.

After waiting a few seconds, Briana finally responded. "I think that would be good for you Nina. I'm truly happy for you...Did you tell Layla yet?" she asked.

"No. She's going to be excited about moving to another place, but she's not going to want to leave her friends and school...I think she'll be ok though. I don't plan to put her in private school in Maryland. We're going to get a nice condo out in the suburbs and she'll go to a good school out there. Really, I'll be able to save more money."

"What are you going to do about your properties and job?"

"I'm going to keep them. And actually I was thinking about letting a property management company handle it. They'll charge me like 30%, but they will handle collecting rent and dealing with maintenance issues...And as far as my job, I work from home now. I'll probably have to drive back a few times a month for meetings but that's not a problem."

"Well you got it figured out Nina. I think you'll do great. Make the move boo," she said, seemingly sincere.

"Thanks Bri...I was thinking...You and Aunt Sheena should come to...Move out of Philly. You could find a job in Baltimore, and I'm sure Aunt Sheena could work at another McDonalds out there, or find something else."

"Girl, I don't know about that...I love Philly. I wanna do hair, and this is the place to be," she said, going back to eating her BLT.

"Well just think about it, ok," I asked.

"I will." Bri looked down at her watch and hopped up. "Oh shit. Therapy session in ten minutes. I have to go to that. Thanks for coming Nina. Let me know how everything goes with the house-hunt." She smiled, and leaned over to give me a hug.

"I will. And I'll be by in a couple of days to check on you."

"Okay..And thanks again Nina."

"Of course sis," I said, with a smile, before getting up from the table and leaving.

Every time I left, Briana said thank you. I really appreciated the gratitude. I had her back and I wanted to help her. I was more so happy she was willing to accept it.

The rehab had set me back $5,000, so I was happy Briana seemed to be getting better. In my eyes, it was worth every penny.

I left Norristown with the intention of stopping downtown to see Nate. My rehabbed properties were just about finished and I wanted to put them on the market as soon as possible. The whole rehab process had been progressing quite smoothly, but I wanted to sell quickly since I would be moving soon.

My goal was to have a place in a month, so by the time Rashid came, everything would be situated. I was going to try to make the move as simple as possible for everyone, including myself. I had so much to do in four weeks, but I was ready.

◇◇◇

The trip to see Nate went better than I had expected. After taking a quick drive to my partially rehabbed properties in Strawberry Mansion, Nate intended to list them both at $39,999. I was cool with the price since I skimped and saved while purchasing materials. I spent way less money than Nate had suggested, so it was only fair that I got back less than he had initially projected for the sale of the two houses.

I didn't care, I just wanted to unload them and make my money back. Nate already had a potential buyer; a couple who were looking to purchase some rental properties. I was excited. This was a new beginning for me, and like Aunt Sheena said, I deserved it.

After leaving Nate, I made a pit stop to North Philly to see Aunt Sheena, since it was her day off. Her birthday was coming up in a few weeks, so I wanted to pick her brain, so I could buy her the perfect gift. I figured I would take her to a late lunch. Nobody loved food more than I, so of course I always wanted to invite people to sit, eat, and talk.

I pulled in front of the house and quickly sent Aunt Sheena a text to let her know I was out front. As I waited I noticed a black Ford Crown Victoria riding slowly up the block. It didn't stop, but something seemed fishy. Since the neighborhood wasn't the best, I dismissed it, and texted, *hurry up*.

I wasn't trying to get caught up in any hood beefs. This was another reason I wanted my aunt to move when I did. I purchased the house for income, but I had no plans or desire to live in it, especially considering it was North Philly. It was a good idea for Aunt Sheena temporarily, but we definitely had to see about getting her out the area.

After another minute, Aunt Sheena came out with a big smile on her face. She had a bun in her head, but was rocking regular blue jeans and a plain black t-shirt. I smiled back at my Aunt, but frowned when I saw the Crown Vic pull back on the block. Just as Aunt Sheena came down the steps and started walking to my car, shots rang out.

I screamed as my aunt hit the ground, while the Crown Vic barreled down the street at full speed. Fear paralyzed me, but once the car turned the block and was gone, reality set in, and I realized I had to help my aunt.

I struggled to get out of the car as adrenaline and panic gripped my body. Blood poured from my Aunt Sheena's arm as she struggled to get up. She had been hit. I screamed internally as I grabbed her and quickly helped her into the car. I ran around to get in the driver's seat so I could get her to the hospital.

"Oh my god! Oh my god!" I cried. "Put pressure on it. Don't let it bleed out." I told Aunt Sheena, so her wound wouldn't leak out as much. I mashed down on the accelerator and headed to Temple Hospital.

"Ahh shit, this shit hurts," she yelled, in pain.

"It's okay Aunt Sheena, I'm gonna get you some help…Shit!" I cried.

Since the hospital wasn't far, I got there in less than five minutes.

I parked directly in front of the Emergency room, and the feeling of déjà vu overcame me. After yanking the passenger door open, I helped my aunt get out of the car, while I yelled for help. People in the waiting room looked at me like I had lost my mind. She had been shot in the arm, so I guess they figured it wasn't that serious. I didn't care though. I didn't live like that, and to us me gun-shot wounds were not the norm.

A couple of nurses ran over to assist, while telling me to stand back. Before I knew it, Aunt Sheena had been taken back in a wheel chair and I was standing there in the ER still in tears. I turned around to go back and move my car, but my vibrating phone in my pocket stopped me. *Another blocked number...I should've know...Naseef's ass.*

I didn't even bother to answer. I already knew what time he was on. I knew the nigga was off, but I definitely underestimated him. I knew Naseef was behind the shooting and I was scared as hell. He knew where I lived and he found the house with no problems. I had told him I owned property but I never showed him where they were.

There was no telling what else he would do or knew. I thought about Layla and Rashid.

SHONTAIYE

Tears streamed down my face. I was fucked. I had gotten Aunt Sheena shot, and I had no choice but to go and tell Rashid. This time it was no one else's bullshit that had gotten me in trouble. No, this was caused by my own lies and deceit. I had spun my own web. Shit was out of hand, and I needed to fix it quick.

TWELVE

IT WAS MIDNIGHT, and I sat on the sofa, waiting for Rashid to respond. He was pissed beyond comprehension.

"Nina why the fuck you ain't been told me this shit?" he asked, jaws clenching. Oh yeah, he was definitely mad.

"I was scared. I thought I could handle him—"

"Ya ass didn't want me to find out you fucked the nigga!" he said, staring at me with disgust.

"Yeah," I said low.

He shook his head, and stood up from the

chair. "So what the fuck you tell the cops?" he asked.

Rashid wanted vengeance, but I wanted to let the cops handle it. I knew it wasn't a ton they could do since we didn't actually see the face of the person or people in the car. I gave them as much information about Naseef as I could, so they could at least question him and lock him up for something; anything.

"I told them what I knew...How I met him...How he's been following me..." I paused before saying the rest. "Where he lives, and the anonymous phone call I got right after taking Aunt Sheena to the hospital." I looked over at Rashid, who was still giving me the look of death.

"Right now they said all they can do is question him, and finally give me the restraining order I requested before." He looked up and glanced over at me.

"How long this shit been going on Nina?" he asked.

I sighed. "I met Naseef before you and I got back together...before we even started seeing each other again."

"But you never ended it when I asked you to?"

"I tried Rashid…I really tried. He wouldn't take no for answer. Once I became firm, he got on some other shit. He popped up on me at the hospital and we exchanged words…After that he went from 0 to 190."

"Where the nigga be at?" he asked.

"Why Rashid…I already told you that the nigga is a killer. That's what he do. He kills for money. I don't want you getting into some shit you not ready for." I regretted putting it in those terms. Rashid looked at me with a bruised ego.

"I can handle whatever, and I'm about whatever," he growled angrily.

Trying to save face, I said, "I know Rashid, but let the cops handle it. That way no one will get in trouble over this bullshit…ok?"

"Aight Nina. Either way, we out…You get on top of the house hunt asap. I ain't scared of no nigga, but I'm scared of what I might have to do to protect my family."

"I will boo…I'ma go check on Aunt Sheena ok?"

"Aight."

I got up and walked to my bedroom where Aunt Sheena was sleep, recovering from the gunshot wound to her arm. Right after she was discharged from the hospital I brought her to my home. There was no way I was letting her step foot back into the apartment. I would gather her things with Rashid later. In the meantime, she was with me.

I peeked out the blinds to see if the patrolman was still stationed outside of the building. Whenever a crime against a person occurred, it was procedure for a cop to sit outside for a day or two for added safety.

As expected, the cop was still stationed in front of the building quietly. I left the room and went into Layla's room to give her a kiss. She too was sleeping peacefully. I didn't plan to send her to school in the morning, or anymore mornings for that matter. I was going to withdraw her and send her back to school in a few weeks when we left for Maryland. I'd rather be safe than sorry. God knows I wouldn't be able to live with myself if something happened to my baby.

I decided I would call Briana in the morning, however, Aunt Sheena made me promise to not tell her what was going on. She felt that is was for the better. With her treatment still in progress, it was best to keep her focused on getting better.

A little while later, I went to my office/guestroom and climbed into the full-size bed. Luckily I had kept it as a guest room, instead of just using it for my office. I wanted Aunt Sheena to be comfortable so I let her have my room. Plus, I had to get back to work in the morning.

I pulled the covers up high to my chin and scooted close to Rashid, wrapping my arm around him. Surprisingly he was still awake. Reaching over, he gently put his hand over my arm.

He didn't have to say anything. His touch told it all. I knew the only reason Rashid was putting up with my bullshit is because he had put me through so much in our past relationship. I wasn't on no tick for tack shit, and I appreciated everything he was doing.

After a few minutes of staring at the soft

black waves in the back of Rashid's head, sleep overcame me.

Two weeks had passed and I was uber excited. Briana had been released from the rehab and was back to her old self. I had found a beautiful condo in a quiet suburb outside of Baltimore, called Glen Burnie. The movers were loading up the last of my things, while I stood in the now empty apartment talking to Briana and my Aunt Sheena.

"I am going to miss you both. Six months is too long," I pouted.

"We gon miss you too, but I gotta wait until the new store opens to leave," Aunt Sheena replied, proudly. She had been offered an opportunity to train as an assistant store manager for a brand new store in Baltimore.

She had asked if she could transfer to be closer to us, but they gave her something better with the new job offer because of her stellar performance. I planned to sweeten the pot right before she moved by buying her a nice used car. I had my eye on a newer model Toyota Corolla. Something nice, and reliable but that wouldn't break the bank. I was extremely proud of her and I wanted to show her. She definitely deserved it, since she literally took a bullet for me.

Thankfully Naseef's ass had been caught on an unrelated shooting. Once he went under investigation for Aunt Sheena's shooting the police spotted him at a bar and were finally able to pull him over for a routine traffic stop. Because of the strong odor of marijuana smoke, they were able to search his car and found a gun that was linked to a previous shooting.

I guess everyone gets caught up behind dumb shit at some point. I hated to find joy in someone else's pain, but I was happy as hell they caught him. I was going to flee Philly undetected and move on with my life. Sad thing was I had genuinely liked Naseef, but he was the true definition of a cold nutcase.

Turning my attention back to Aunt Sheena, I wrapped my arms around her and gave her a big hug.

"I'm proud of you Aunt Sheena. I love

you," I gushed.

"Thank you baby," she replied. Releasing her I switched my focus to Briana.

"I'm proud of you too Briana. This has been a long hard year for you, but you kicked through it. You've been through a lot and you proved your strength." I released her and wiped a tear from my eye. They were about to leave, and soon I was too. Layla and I were going to be getting on the road in an hour and head to our new home. It was bitter sweet, but I knew it was best.

I had to pat myself on the back, because in two short weeks I had found us a home, sold two investment properties, and found a property management company to manage my remaining properties. Things were going well, and the last thing I needed to do was transfer some money from my old bank to a smaller, local bank in Maryland.

After watching the movers load up the remaining items and head to Maryland, I slowly got in my car with Layla to head to the bank before we began the drive. I looked back at the apartment building and sighed. I would miss this place.

It was amazing how one negative event could damn near ruin your day. Walking out of the Bank of America, I took a few deep breaths to keep from flipping out. I had went there to withdraw a large sum of money but they told me they could only give me $5,000 in cash. I didn't understand how I had several hundred thousand dollars in that bank but they could only manage to scrape up $5,000 to give me. *Talking about they were low on bills. That wasn't my damn problem.*

After raising hell, which didn't get me anywhere I took the money and left. I made a mental note to cancel the account completely and take my business elsewhere. Had it been an emergency I would have been shit out of luck. And to think I was going to leave a little something in there.

I texted Rashid and let him know we were en route to the new house and he immediately texted back a smiley face. He would be joining us in a month and I couldn't wait. Layla was especially happy when we told her mommy and daddy would be giving it another shot. Our family was complete and there was nothing that could stop us.

THIRTEEN

3 months later

"I DON'T KNOW Aunt Sheena. At the last minute, she called and said she wasn't coming yesterday. She said she would get on the first train this morning. I called her and she didn't answer. She hasn't been answering all day," I said, worried.

Three months had passed since we had gotten settled in our new condo, and I had invited Aunt Sheena and Briana to visit. Aunt Sheena came as planned but Briana was a no show, and now wasn't answering the phone.

"I don't know what's going on, but I'm

worried. Everything seemed fine with her. She seemed normal. She was working down at the Weave Bar washing hair, and she was supposed to start hair school in a month." She shook her head before saying, "I'm going back tomorrow. I wanna make sure everything is okay with her."

"No Aunt Sheena. I'm sure she's fine. If we don't hear from her, then we can both drive over to Philly."

"You can't be doing all that traveling Nina. You're five months pregnant," Rashid butted in from across the room.

"I know Rashid, but I gotta check on Briana."

"Briana's a big girl. I'm sure she's fine, but you gotta make sure you chill on the running around and stress," he added.

As much as I hated to admit, he was right. Shortly after arriving in Maryland, I discovered I was eight weeks pregnant. The bouts of tiredness were finally explained. Rashid and Layla were super excited, and I can't lie, I was too.

"Well I can take the train back. I can't rest

knowing that something could be wrong," Aunt Sheena said. I could see the worry on her face. We all were worried.

"Okay Aunt Sheena. If that makes you rest better, then I'll buy and print the ticket first thing in the morning...But I'm sure she's fine."

"I just have a funny feeling Nina." I prayed she was wrong.

The morning finally came and we still hadn't heard a word from Bri. As promised, I purchased Aunt Sheena a ticket so she could go back to Philly to check on her. She had two weeks off, so she would return in a few days.

With swollen feet I walked to the night stand to get my keys so I could run Aunt Sheena down to the train station. Before my hand could grip them up, I heard a knock at the door.

That was probably Briana. Maybe her phone had died, or she had gotten lost. I told her I would pick her up from the train station when we planned the visit, but she insisted she catch a cab since I was pregnant.

Snatching the door open, I didn't bother to look out the peephole. My heart sank when I didn't see my sister at the door. Instead, I saw two white men in cheap suits and another uniformed police officer.

"Hi. Are you Nina Washington?" the older of the two men asked. He had gray hair, and had on a gray suit that made him appear washed out.

"That's me…And you are?" I asked, becoming a bit nervous as Aunt Sheena walked up behind me. I hoped nothing was wrong with Briana.

"I'm Officer Richard Franklin with the United States Government, and we're here to issue an arrest warrant for you. You are under arrest for tax fraud, and evasion."

"Oh my god," I said, as my throat immediately dried up and my head started spinning. I looked at Aunt Sheena, and told her to call Rashid.

Turning me around, the uniformed officer grabbed my wrists and placed cold metal cuffs over them. I knew when I walked out of the door that it would be a while before I stepped foot back through them. I was glad Rashid and Layla weren't there so they didn't have to see me like this, but I was also sad because I wouldn't be able to kiss them goodbye.

A year later, after pleading guilty to tax fraud, and tax evasion I was sentenced to two years house arrest. The legal fees to get that sentence nearly crippled Rashid and me for the year I fought the case.

Through the turmoil I managed to give birth to a beautiful, healthy baby boy named Isaiah. He was the main reason I was able to get two years house arrest instead of doing it in a federal penitentiary. All of my rental properties were seized, my bank account were frozen, and I was neutralized down to nothing.

Turned out that Briana had been running her mouth to a so called friend, and once they had a falling out, her friend blabbed to the IRS. My so called sister in turn, ratted me out to take the heat off of herself.

I ended up losing my job since there was no way I would be able to continue holding a position in the fraud department when I had a federal fraud conviction.

Despite all the adversity, I still wasn't bitter. I had a beautiful family and Aunt Sheena had even moved in during my legal woes to help with expenses. She had finally gotten the courage to wash her hands of Briana. She said she couldn't let her tear down everyone. Last we heard, she had gotten six months.

One day my sister and I would eventually cross paths again, and I would smile. You see, I wasn't stupid by a long shot. I knew there was always a possibility that this could happen, especially after the blackmailing incident. After taking my properties and seizing my cash out of my accounts, I had managed to pay off a good amount of what the Feds said I owed. What I did still owe, I made payment arrangements over five years to pay off the remaining balance.

Despite all the bullshit I had been through, once my probation and house arrest were over,

I decided the whole family was taking a much needed vacation to the Cayman Islands. I had a nice fat hidden bank account there that the Feds couldn't see or touch. I would always think ahead. I would always come out on top.

◇◇◇

ENJOYED THIS BOOK. PLEASE LEAVE A REVIEW OR RATING.

◇◇◇

ALSO CHECK OUT MY OTHER TITLE FOR FREE: *DECEIT, LIES, & ALIBI'S* FREE

◇◇◇

HERE'S A SNEAK PEAK...

Coming Soon FREE for a limited time: DECEIT, LIES, AND ALIBI'S

Meet Noah...

Handsome and orphaned Noah grew up poor like most kids from North Philly. Refusing to accept poverty as his fate, he along with his childhood friend Hakim, jacked their way to the top. Years later, he's on a legal path and building a future with his beloved fiancée Shaleea. However when slick talking Eve comes into the picture, love triangles form and everything that Noah has is threatened. Friends are foes, everyone is out for self, and loyalty is no more. As love and lust intertwine, tempers flare and life changing mistakes are made. The stakes are high in this hood tale filled with deceit, lies, and alibis.

Sneak Peek of
DECEIT, LIES, AND ALIBI'S

Chapter 1

Present day

Noah saw his former life flash before his eyes as he stood over Eve with his hands wrapped around her throat. He thought of all that he had, and all that his life was before her scheming ass had come into the picture. He cursed the day he had met her. Instead of his surroundings, he saw nothing but red through his pupils. The sounds she made became muffled and distant. Noah's heart beat rapidly and before he realized it, he had completely blacked out. It was too late.

18 months ago
Eve

It was four a.m. and Eve had been on her computer for several hours. This was her work time and she was in grind mode. She was used to staying up till the wee hours of the morning updating her profile on different internet sites. Eve was an escort and earned her money by having sex with men, however, she liked to consider herself an entertainer. She frequently told people she was a dancer, since she wouldn't dare tell them she was an escort or prostitute.

She continued to work on uploading her most recent photos, being careful to select those that highlighted her most popular attributes: her tiny waist and fat ass. Eve wasn't traditionally pretty. She had strong facial features that sometimes made her appear a bit masculine, however, her Haitian heritage gave her somewhat of an exotic look. With some makeup and sexy clothes she certainly managed to make many men's heads turn. After all, she had to attract men; they were here bread and butter, and the only way she knew how to survive.

Eve wasn't dealt the greatest hand in life. One of four children to an illiterate, immigrant single mother, Eve had always been poor. Eve's mother had migrated with her siblings to America when Eve was just the tender age of 15. With a poor economy, no education, and little skill to obtain a job, Eve's mother Rosa struggled to raise her four children. Back in Haiti, she had relied on prostitution to care for them.

When Eve became old enough, she too turned to prostitution to earn money. She thought back to her early teenage years in Haiti when she used to sleep with white men who came to trade goods on their boats. Eve's body had developed very early, and in her adolescent years she had a body many grown women envied. Men and boys alike loved her dark chocolate skin, her full lips, and her thick thighs and ass. The first time she took goods in exchange for her own "goods" she was 12 years old. She remembered the day...

It was hot, and the sun beamed heavily on her small back. She was hungry and her mother had sent her down to the trading pier with a few dollars. She was hoping she could use the money to get a loaf of bread to go with a pot of broth her mother had been trying to prepare. They were desperate, and their food supply was beginning to run out. Rosa was getting older, and because of a poor diet and lack of proper medical care, her looks and health were deteriorating quickly. She could no longer sway the white traders with propositions of sex, so she sent Eve.

When Eve arrived at the boat she knew what she had to do. With a seductive smile and a lustful tone, she told a middle-age, white trader what she wanted. She then explained to him she only had a few dollars, however, she had something else more valuable than money. The trader knew exactly what she spoke of, and frankly he didn't mind a bit. He smiled back at the young Eve, and she knew she had him.

"Follow me," he said. "You take care of me and I'll take care of you."

So she did just that. Many times Eve had listened to her mother and even spied on her and countless men having sex. Although still a virgin, she knew exactly what to say and do, to satisfy a man. When Eve got to the back of the boat she wasted no time straddling the aging white man on the small makeshift sleeping area. She told him to close his eyes and then she kissed him softly on his chest and neck.

She pulled open his shirt and proceeded to rub his shoulders. She didn't want to spend too much time on the boat so she decided to get down to business. She eased down the traders pants and took him deep into her mouth. She ignored the smell of old sweat and focused on making him cum quickly. She bobbed her head up and down swiftly, sucking furiously, while making loud slurping sounds.

"Ummmmmm," she moaned. "You're so big," she said between slurps, hoping to get him off quickly. That too she had learned from watching her

mother.

As soon as she purred the words he came violently, grabbing her hair, his body twitching. He was done, and she praised herself for being skilled enough to get him off so quickly.

When it was all over, Eve had enough to last her and her family several days. Her services to the fisherman became routine, and eventually spread amongst the other traders. Thus a monster had just been created.

When Eve's mother announced she had gotten a family visa to America, Eve was ecstatic. She thought her days of prostitution, hunger, and poverty were all over. However, when they got to America she was in for a rude awakening. The area of Brooklyn they lived in was poverty stricken and crime ridden. What made things worse was that her mother spoke broken English and had no education, so she had difficulty getting a job.

They eventually moved to the projects and lived off the welfare system, receiving food stamps and a small assistance check. Eve became extremely envious when saw the other teenage girls her age who were pretty, and well dressed. She wanted what they had, so she began to scheme for months.

One month when check day came, Eve wasted no time going through her mother's purse to find her EBT card so she could take the $750 that would post on the card at midnight. After taking the money from the ATM, she returned her mother's card and headed out into the night. Although she felt guilty she had taken the money, she wasn't concerned that they would be evicted. Their rent was only $30 a month, and she could have that to her in no time. Besides, her mother received over $1000 a month in food-stamps; she would have no problem selling a few in exchange for cash.

Eve used the money to rent a room in a cheap motel for a week. The following day she also went to the nearest hair salon for some extensions. Her final splurge was a quality camera phone. To her, the money spent was an investment. She would use the camera phone to take sexy pictures of herself and post them to the Internet on some escort websites she was hearing about. Fucking was going to be her hustle in the State's too.

The prostitution game had changed. Long gone were the days of standing on the corner waving down cars, and sucking dick in pissy alleyways. That method was more so for drug addicts. Younger girls were now getting money off "the game" by setting up shop in cleaner, more discreet environments such as motel rooms.

Perverts and dirty old men were no longer the only clients; business men, regular working men, and just about anyone was paying for sex. Several girls she knew were making good money, and Eve wanted a piece of the pie.

The first site she heard about, Backpage.com, would eventually become her favorite. She used it religiously along with Escorts.com. Those two sites were where ninety-five percent of her income came from; that and word of mouth. All she had to do was pay a small advertising fee so she could solicit her services to men looking for sex. It really was a win-win situation for her.

Within weeks Eve had men coming in and out of her room. She made enough to have fun, keep her makeup and hair flawless, and keep the latest threads. She actually made a decent income when you considered what she paid to practically live out of motels.

Eventually Eve went to visit her mother to apologize and pay her money back. Although she had been gone for weeks, her mother never worried or questioned her whereabouts. It wasn't unusual for girls to run off at eleven and twelve in Haiti.

Eve told her mother she had a part-time job at a fast food restaurant. She didn't tell her what she was really doing or how much money she was making because she didn't want her begging for handouts. Deep down Eve resented her mother.

Long ago her mother had been married to a decent Haitian man who was also the father of her first three children. When Eve's mother got pregnant a fourth time, rumors were swirling around the village that the unborn child did not belong to her husband. For years her mother had been known for her promiscuity amongst the people of the small community. Nevertheless, the creamy skin of the half Caucasian baby confirmed the rumors when she gave birth. Soon after, her husband left and never returned.

Eve felt that her mother had her chance in life and blew it. Because of her failures, her children suffered and lived miserably, forced to turn tricks and suck old, white dicks just to eat.

Eve refused to be a miserable, failure like her mother. Problem was, that was all she knew. However, Eve felt that if she had to suck dick to make a living she would focus on sucking the right dick. Sadly, she had grown up so ignorant she never knew that if she pursued a proper education she could have had a future. Even if Eve had known, she probably wouldn't have done it anyway. She instead, kept her mind on three things: men, money, and dick.

She hoped to find someone who was paid and that would eventually take her in and provide for her. She met few men she felt were good candidates. Most of them were too old, too broke, or married. Those that were married usually just wanted fun and wouldn't even think of leaving their wives. She couldn't wait till she finally met "The One." Little did she know that he was on his way, and she would eventually get a whole lot more than what she had bargained for.

Chapter 2

Noah

"Yo, bull," Noah mouthed into the receiver of his iPhone 5, greeting his child-hood friend Hakim.

"Wassup my nigga," replied Hakim, still focused on whipping his Cadillac Deville in and out of mid-day traffic.

"We still going up-top tonight to celebrate?" Noah asked.

"No doubt, my dude," Hakim responded, holding his phone up with his shoulder since his hands were occupied by the steering wheel.

"Pick me up around 8 and we out. Oh, and grab some of that good shit," he said, referring to the exotic weed they both liked to smoke.

"No doubt. I got you. It's ya day. Everything's on me," Noah replied, with a smile.

"Good looking my nigga. See you then. One."

Hakim ended the call and allowed his phone to drop into the plush leather seats.

The two friends went back to their tasks and began to mentally prepare for the two and a half hour drive from Philadelphia to New York. It was Hakim's birthday and after living in Philly for most of his adolescent years, he decided that their club scene just didn't compare to his home-town New York, so he asked Noah to accompany him there for a party being thrown in honor of his birthday.

Noah pulled his Polo hoodie tight against his body for extra warmth against the brisk air. It was surprisingly cold for April, but that didn't stop him from standing outside of his door, blunt in hand, blowing smoke circles into the air. He couldn't smoke in the house because his fiancé Shaleea wouldn't allow it. He adored Shaleea and was always willing to compromise with her to make life smooth. They'd been together 7 years and he'd taken her through hell and back during that time, but she still stuck by him.

Four months prior he officially declared his love by proposing to her on Christmas Eve with a five carat, princess cut diamond ring. It had set him back $10,000, but he gladly paid it since she was worth every penny. She truly was one in a million.

Shaleea was beautiful to him, with smooth skin that resembled fudge. She had a loving and caring personality, and it didn't hurt that she was educated. What really made his love run deep for her was that she wasn't like all the other girls that came and went in his life; she truly cared for him as a person and never worried about his money, or what she could gain from being with him. Her love for him was pure. She listened when he talked, gave him sound advice, and was affectionate. He wouldn't deny that she was good to him.

"Ouch!" Noah winced in pain. While deep in thought, he had smoked his blunt down so low it burned his hand. Throwing down the "roach" and smashing it up with his Timberland boot, he decided he was done. He opened up the oversized cherry-wood door to return back into his modest town-home. He was finally ready to begin preparation for his night out in New York for Hakim's birthday. He was eager to unwind and let loose in the city. Just like his favorite rapper Drake, YOLO was his motto. *"You only live once."*

No doubt he loved Shaleea and wanted to spend the rest of his life with her, but at the end of the day he was a man. Noah felt like it just wasn't in the nature of man to be faithful. *Bend them over, fuck em, and get em out*, was how he went about dealing with hoes. Every now and then if the head game and sex was right, he would toss a few dollars, but none of them would ever get anything close to what he gave to Shaleea; his heart.

Chapter 3

Shaleea

At 8am the cobblestone streets of Chestnut Hill were congested and already bustling with activity. The neighborhood, which was nestled in the Northwest section of Philadelphia, was home to upper middle class residents and had homes that averaged around $600,000.

Struggling through traffic down the bumpy road, 28 year old Shaleea had just dropped her daughter Heaven off at school and was on her way to get a hot cup of coffee from Dunkin Donuts. That was her energy during the week. She needed a caffeinated boost so she could finish writing a paper on Ethics for her graduate class at Temple University. After finishing her paper she would make her rounds to the four laundromat's she and her fiancé Noah owned; Squeaky Clean; one, two, three, and four.

Four years ago, Shaleea had finally gotten Noah to invest some money into a legitimate business for them to build their future together on. They initially opened one small, run-down, 24-hour laundromat in North Philadelphia with $50,000. Noah was a little hesitant to put the money up at first, not wanting to invest too much. As much money as he had tucked away, he certainly was frugal.

With some convincing, Shaleea was able to instill confidence in Noah and let her show him she was capable of running a business. It wasn't that he didn't believe in her; Noah just wasn't into taking monetary losses.

Although the laundromat was run-down, Shaleea saw the potential because of the location. With the help of a few crack-head's and contractors, they had the place looking presentable in no time. To their delight the business did wonderfully. With an aggressive investment strategy in place, they had been able to open a new location every year.

The businesses thrived in the poor neighborhoods of Philadelphia where most families couldn't afford the luxury of having a washer or dryer in their home. Although the laundromat's were in the ghetto, Shaleea focused on making them affordable and comfortable, using her own money she had saved to offer Wi-Fi, air-conditioning, cable television, and free store-bought muffins and fresh coffee. Her goal was to create a professional establishment people wouldn't mind sitting in for several hours while they did their laundry.

Many businesses in urban areas such as North Philly, were ran down and un-kept. She felt poor people deserved decent, clean businesses in their neighborhood just like anyone else. So far, the hard work had paid off and their laundromats were extremely successful, bringing them in a net profit of around $40 thousand per month before expenses.

She hoped to soon convince Noah to open up additional locations in Baltimore. The goal was to capitalize off the urban market by expanding in the inner city. She wanted to be like George and Weezie.

With Shaleea proving her business skills and intelligence, Noah no longer hesitated to hand her his bank card or give her a blank check. In time, she no longer needed his cash to grow; she had her own, along with joint credit cards, and bank accounts.

Shaleea was the brains in the relationship. She had a Bachelor's degree in Finance and was on her way to obtaining an MBA from Temple University. Noah was the muscle and the money, not necessarily earning his small fortune, but taking it through brute force through a small team he and Hakim founded called Torch Boyz.

In the past, Noah didn't discriminate. He started off robbing people as well as small establishments. He eventually moved on to more lucrative capers such as check cashing places, and ultimately bank ATM's. Noah liked to describe himself as peaceful during his dirty deeds. However, in the event that anyone decided to be a tough guy, he would quickly show them he was in charge. He did his best to avoid hurting innocent people, however, that was sometimes inevitable, especially if there was any threat posed against him or his well-being.

Noah and Hakim robbed for many years. As time went on they focused on the quality and not the quantity, targeting ATM's in various cities throughout the country that were known to hold up to a hundred thousand dollars at once. Over time, several ATM's in a night quickly put the pair where they wanted to be financially.

Those days however, were in the past. No longer wild and reckless, Noah was now a businessman who hoped to grow his businesses and expand his portfolio to soon include real estate. He was extremely stable financially and had a decent amount of "old" money he wanted to invest. He was in love with Shaleea and ready to fully settle down and make her his wife. He also longed for a family and hoped he would eventually achieve that with Shaleea and Heaven.

Noah had lost his mother and father to the streets when he was seven years old. His dad Boogie had been a well-known jack boy in the city. He was known to do whatever necessary to take care of his baby boy and baby-mama. He also had a reputation as being merciless and deadly. However, after years of providing for his family by taking from others, he eventually found himself on the opposite end of the gun.

Boogie and his girl Pam, Noah's mother, were brutally gunned down in their home late one cold, December night. Police never made any arrests. However, word on the street was someone killed him out of revenge.

After Noah lost his parents he found himself in and out of foster homes longing for a stable family. He sincerely appreciated Shaleea and Heaven because of the stability they gave him. He felt God gave them to him so he could be whole again; and he did indeed feel whole.

Shaleea had met Noah 7 years back in the Germantown section of Philadelphia. She had just purchased a seafood platter from the Velvet Lounge, and was walking back to her car on Chelten Avenue. Her deep Hershey colored skin, along with her shapely figure is what caught Noah's eye as she walked to her small Honda civic parked up the street.

Shaleea had hips that literally stuck out on her voluptuous frame and complemented her heart shaped bottom. Noah was in awe since he'd always been a sucker for a nice body. When he approached her she seemed a bit hesitant to converse with the handsome stranger who stood before her, however his charm eventually put her at ease.

At 6 foot 1, Noah towered over Shaleea's 5 foot 4 curvy stature. He was boy next door handsome with big round eyes that were mysterious and hinted at a dark past. He wore a sharp, low cut Caesar hairstyle, and a full beard around a mouth that revealed a row of shiny white teeth. He had a caramel complexion and a boyish grin that mesmerized and captivated her. She was intrigued by the stranger.

After introducing themselves to one another the two immediately hit it off, standing on the sidewalk talking for almost an hour. They eventually exchanged numbers, with her watching him walk off.

She noticed he was walking as she drove off so she assumed he didn't have a car and used public transportation. In actuality, his car was parked several blocks away and he was simply walking to reach it. Although she didn't know this, she was never bothered by the fact of him using public transportation. She was far from superficial and shallow, having been taught as a child that materials didn't define the man.

Her father was a hardworking man who didn't have a lot of money. However, he had a lot of love in his heart and he was a provider. Shaleea felt that if she could find a good man with a good heart, that's all she would need in this world. Her mother had taught her that behind every good man is a good woman; security and stability would come along with it if they worked together as a team. She didn't mind working and doing her part.

Her mother had worked in nursing as long as Shaleea could remember. She was a strong woman who never received welfare. She stood on her own, and made sure she instilled those values in her four girls. *"No man wants a lazy dumb woman,"* her mother would tell them. *"A beautiful hard working woman is valuable to a man."*

Unfortunately Shaleea's father Tate didn't realize that in the beginning. While he was a good provider, he was a dog who liked to often stray away from home. When Shaleea's mom Gina found out, she left him. She stood on her own since then, never asking him for anything except to take care of his daughters. Luckily for Gina, she was still young and later found a good man named Chris who drove trucks for a living and earned a respectable salary.

To Shaleea, Gina and Chris embodied the American dream of love and success. They weren't rich but they were stable and financially secure; that's the only thing Shaleea wanted.

ABOUT THE AUTHOR

Shontaiye is a bookstore-library freak. She is an avid reader who was blessed with a vivid and active imagination since she was a small child.

She has a Bachelor's in Business and works in emergency services at a large company in Delaware.

When she's not creating fictitious characters, she's going to graduate school for a Master's in Communication. She currently resides by the beach in Maryland, with her daughter and husband. This is her third novel.